T

Also by David Wojnarowicz:

The Waterfront Journals

David Wojnarowicz

Edited by Amy Scholder

Grove Press
New York

The editor wishes to thank Tom Rauffenbart.

Published simultaneously in Canada
Printed in the United States of America

Library of Congress Cataloging-in-Publication Data
Wojnarowicz, David.
The waterfront journals / by David Wojnarowicz; introduction by Tony Kushner. —1st ed.
p. cm.
ISBN 978-0-8021-3504-9

1. United States—Social life and customs—20th century—Fiction.
2. Gay men—Travel—United States—Fiction. 3. Character sketches.
4. Monologues. I. Title.
PS3573.044W38   1996   813'.54—dc20   95-45735

DESIGN BY LAURA HAMMOND HOUGH

Grove Press
154 West 14th Street
New York, NY 10011

Contents

Editor's Preface

On February 20, 1989, David Wojnarowicz sent me his manuscript *The Waterfront Journals*. I was fascinated by these monologues, as David called them, and asked to see more. He set them aside to focus on current writings and to give public readings. The new work was published in his first book, *Close to the Knives,* by Random House in 1991. We discussed another project, one that would combine his drawings and watercolors with text. *Memories That Smell Like Gasoline* was published in 1992 by Artspace Books. In the process of putting together that publication, David found in his notebooks an early draft of "From the Diaries of a Wolf Boy," which is now the final story in *The Waterfront Journals.* Many of the monologues had been published over the years in small magazines, chapbooks, and anthologies. David intended to work on *The Waterfront Journals* as his next literary project, but then he became ill. He had written them before he had AIDS, before becoming an AIDS activist, before establishing himself as a painter, photographer, video maker, and performance artist. They are from a time in his life when he hitchhiked, looked for sex anywhere, and talked to strangers. Before he died, David and I discussed how these early writings might be received. He thought people wouldn't believe these characters existed in the world. He felt that AIDS had so completely changed him that this evidence of his former self would surprise those who knew only his later work. He felt it revealed his romanticism, his idealism, his orientation to the world before rage and hopelessness set in. After he died, on July 22, 1992, I found the letter he sent me with his manuscript in 1989. He signed off: "I wrote this book over the last thirteen or fourteen years. It's all true."

Amy Scholder
August 1995
New York City

Introduction

BY TONY KUSHNER

Americans imagine a protective distance between ourselves and the lives lived on our city streets. Street life occupies another world, another realm of experience, night to our daytime, a furtive shadow city where different rules and ethics apply, inhabited by beings many of us secretly regard as less than fully human. It's an essential trope of all those gritty cop shows on TV, of all the newest crop of neo-noir movies: The life of the street is our lives' antithesis, its criminality and dysfunctionality contrasting appealingly with what we choose to call our decency and sanity. We pass daily through this alter world untouched (except when we are assaulted by it). Only the police, we tell ourselves, hold dual citizenship, only the police can cross the border and come back again. Their martial force, their eager, sanctioned violence is their passport and safe-conduct into the streets and then home again; that's why we employ them. Only the police can descend into Hell, harrow it, and return. We, the proud citizens of a democracy, imagine ourselves incapable of this border crossing, can only conceive of life lived in the open, in public spaces, as being fugitive-invisible, corrupting, enshrouded in mystery, a danger to us. This is telling, and one thing I think it tells us is that we have been successfully inculcated with a fear of the political potential of public space.

David Wojnarowicz lived a substantial and formative part of his life on the street, which is to say in public, which is also to say *before the public, in view*, and this might explain why his work is possessed of such a profound and electrifying theatricality. It's become a mantra of conservatives and liberals alike to decry the theatricalization of public discourse, a way of lamenting that our engagement with life has become artificial, shallow, cheap. Phenomena across the political spectrum—everything from the Reagan presidency to ACT UP—are criticized as being excessively theatrical. But this lamentation is predicated upon a misunderstanding of the theatrical. Really, *all* public discourse is theatrical, in the sense that in all public speech, in all public rhetoric and debate, there is an active, generative tension between partisan power posturing, between strategically designed *effect,* and the truth as one knows it. It's chimeric to seek to rid civic debate and public life of theatricality, of performance consciousness, which is one of the political irreducibles. To exist *in public* demands performance. This is not new to the awful times in which we live, nor is it a cause or symptom of their awfulness. The creepy thing about Reagan, I think, is not that he was an actor who theatricalized politics—the political *is* theatrical, and vice versa—but rather that out of his dreadful politics he made very bad theater. Reaganite theater was a theater of a waxworks politesse, a theater of mausoleum hush, of cemetery calm. In denying the presence of terror, it could never provoke pity; it was all strokes and no catharsis. Any-one who's stood facing a Wojnarowicz painting or print, anyone who's encountered the irresistible, heart-racing rage and beauty of his writing, knows that here was a civic, politi-cal art of an entirely other order.

In the monologues gathered in this book, David Wojnaro-wicz offers and provokes anger over brutality, degradation, exploitation, and oppression, and he decries the complicity of our social order in creating and perpetuating such condi-tions. His indignation and indictment are embodied and im-plicit in the voices he's chosen to remember, record, re-create. He collapses safe distances and separations, he erases the border by simply refusing to acknowledge it. The speaking floor is given over in these fictions to people who seldom have the chance to speak to a listening audience; Wojnarowicz manages to frame an accusation of the social structures to which such lives are subject without committing the socio-logical sin of objectifying them or zoologizing the people who have lived them. His characters become both the authors of their narratives and the performers.

In John Carlin's essay "David Wojnarowicz: As the World Turns," included in *Tongues of Flame*, the artist is linked convincingly and usefully to Emerson and Whitman and the nineteenth-century search for what Carlin calls "an entirely new theory of vision integrally combined with one of repre-sentation." In *The Waterfront Journals* as well as in other work, Wojnarowicz seeks, with incredible subtlety, to show both the world and what it means, to make brute facts di-vulge their hidden truths. So one is heartbroken and appalled, as one ought to be, by the terrible hardships and betrayals presented in this book; also one is moved by the realization that is, for me at least, the book's great cumulative impact: the persistence, even in the face of horror, of an understanding and a demand for justice. That this cry for justice is made articulate without a trace of sentimentality is only further proof, as if we needed further proof, of the great talent, even perhaps the genius, of the author.

Recently *The New York Times* published a beautiful encomium to John Keats on the two hundredth anniversary of his death, by the poet Philip Levine. Writing this introduction, I was in a mood to pay attention to the parallels between Keats's tragically short, incredibly hard life and David Wojnarowicz's, and I don't think the comparison at all far-fetched. While we will not know what the future will make of the work any of us are doing, it is absolutely true of Wojnarowicz what Levine writes of Keats: "I've thought so many times . . . of the poems that might have been ours and the enormous literary reputation that might have been his, had John Keats lived his three score and ten." Both artists died much too soon. And as Levine does in Keats's, I see in Wojnarowicz's art an attempt "to account for the function of pain and suffering in the creation of the human spirit." To describe the art this way is not to ignore the extent to which Wojnarowicz's painting, photography, performance, and writing also constitute a courageous, blazing rejection of the necessity and inevitability of pain and suffering; I don't want to strip the work of its manifest political content and intent. But the transmutation of suffering into wisdom must be accounted among humanity's redemptive possibilities. And I have always found such possibility powerfully conjured up in the art of David Wojnarowicz.

* * *

All of which is to say that the loss of an artist of this importance is a staggering blow to the world at a time when the world can ill afford it. Wojnarowicz's best work, its generosity and abundance, and the breadth of his talents approach something like genius; certainly he wrote truer, finer, more wrenching and awakening things about injustice, sex, resistance, love, and dying than almost anyone writing today. *The Waterfront Journals* returns us to the harsh, gorgeous, revivifying light that falls everywhere on his world. It was written during a time of savage Reaction, the time in which its author lived, and even now, with the savagery increasing exponentially with every passing day, the fact of such vision promises the possibility and proclaims the urgency of resistance.

The Waterfront Journals

Man in Harbor Coffee Shop

SAN FRANCISCO

When I was in prison there were these two brothers, Hugh and Roy D'Autremont, who I became good friends with. I don't know if you ever heard of them but they were in prison for life for blowing up an entire train to get the mail-car money. So every day I'd walk with Hugh in the yard ... he was like this great mystical teacher but without getting into the mysticism, just a beautiful fella. So we'd walk along and stop every now and then because he had something to say to me like: Earl, do you see that guard tower? and I'd say, Yeah, and he'd say: Well take your fingers and measure how big it is from here, and I'd take my thumb and forefinger and place them about an inch apart so that the guard tower fit neatly between the two, and Hugh would say: Got it? and I'd say, Yeah, and he'd say without taking his eyes off the guard tower: That's how high it really is. Then we'd talk awhile more while I pondered this and realized he was talking about perspective ... and every so often we'd pass his brother Roy and Hugh would say: My pawn to your bishop, like they were playing mental chess, didn't even have a chessboard, they knew each position of the pieces in their heads which means Hugh was teaching me things and talking about various subjects and all the while he'd be pondering the moves of the chess game in his head . . .

I had a lot of great sex in prison . . . there was always some guy at my elbow trying to persuade me to drop whatever daddy I had and go with him . . . there was one time that I had two guys at once. One was a real handsome guy but he had had a prefrontal lobotomy. Whenever we would get into conversations about the past he could only remember up to a certain point, then he'd explain his loss of memory with: That's when they cut off my horns. So I was making it with him and at the same time I was making it with this other fella who was in for murder. One day I was sewing in my cell when this queen rushed up and said: Earl, Earl. Joe and Butch are out there killing each other. They found out you've been making it with both of them! So I quick rushed into the yard and there they were punching it out and I ran up and got in between them and said: Now boys you stop fighting this instant . . . you both should know better . . . why there's surely enough of me to go around. Well after that they both thought about it and I was dropped . . . neither of them would see me anymore . . .

Guy on Second Avenue
1:00 A.M.

NEW YORK CITY

This friend of mine was up in Central Park on the West Side around Seventy-fifth Street or somethin like that and he was walking around in the park by the Rambles in this area with lots of trees and overgrown paths and he's cruisin and at some point this good-looking guy walks by him real slow and they check each other out and the guy passes him with a heavy cruise and continues on and my friend turns around and watches him go into this small clearing surrounded by hilly slopes where there's a circle of benches and it's night and dark as hell but the circle is lit up with lampposts and the guy sits down and looks for him so my friend turns and starts walking towards the smiling guy sitting on the bench and he's about to enter the circle and suddenly out the corner of his eye he sees something on the hillside move and he looks around and there's about seven dark-skinned guys black or Haitian moving down the hill from all different directions towards the guy sitting in the pool of light on one bench looking towards him smiling and so my friend turns around and yells Run run run and starts running

like hell the short distance across the field towards this huge
stone wall about eight feet high separating the park from the
street and he's running like hell and he jumps up on top of
this series of boulders and leaps over to the wall catching it
and pulling himself over onto the street and he looks down
as he does so and there's this one black guy standing beneath the wall looking up at him and he's got a knife in his
hand and then he looks out over the field to the circle of
benches and at that moment the seven other guys have
reached the guy sitting on the bench and they close in on
him and my friend says he sees them all lift their hands in
the air simultaneously and the knives come down stabbing
him over and over and there's not a sound and he turns and
runs to a police station and reports what's happened and a
couple cops take him out there in their car and they get to
the clearing and there's no sign of nothin no sign of the guy
who cruised him or the other guys no sign of a struggle and
he can't explain it to the cops and he goes home and a week
later the cops call him up and ask him to come downtown
and make a possible identification of a male head found in
the park and he goes and it's the guy who smiled at him one
night a week ago and he talked with a number of people and
found out it mighta been some voodoo cult and he flipped
out so he gets this tattoo on his wrist to protect himself and
he disappears for a while and a year later I seen him and he
seemed different invisible so that you might not notice him
if you passed him on the street . . .

Guy in Waterfront Hotel

SAN FRANCISCO

See here on this map ... I was born in Austin Texas ... see right here ... my father had me seeing the bishop all the time. I was a very religious child. So I go to the bishop and ask him certain questions about god and he says Now Gordon, we won't have people doubting their god. I said What? I'm asking questions because I want to learn not because I doubt ... one time the bishop was talking about gay people ... I'd never known what they were ... I was a pretty quiet kid, you know, didn't know anything, so when I heard what he was saying about them I thought what's wrong with them for doing that? ... so I went downtown and into the Gulch Bar ... Gulch Bar Gulch Restaurant Gulch Bakery everything in that town was called Gulch ... so I went into the Gulch Bar and picked me up a cowboy and I told him what I wanted him to do to me and we went right home and did it ... ha ha ha ... when the bishop found out he was upset. He said Boy you have an authority problem. Me? An authority problem? ... ha ha ha ... so that's when my father moved us up to Colorado ... see this line I've drawn on the map? well from here my brother was sent into the army ... then my father was sent over to Pennsylvania in order to work and he died ... the next thing I know my mother's on the phone talking to god knows who saying You promised me that when his father died you would get him work. She was talking about me of course ... that bitch she knew what was going to happen ... and the next thing I know I'm in Salt Lake City surrounded by Mormons and they're handing me my robe. Now I don't know how I got there but I became a Mormon which takes me from here to there ... see the direction the lines are moving in? well after three months of being a Mormon I called up my mother and said Mom I just saw people melting on the street. I was walking down the street in Salt Lake City and people were vanishing left and right so I called my mother and told her and do you know what she said? She said Gordon don't let it upset you. They're not there they're not real ... ha ha ha ... So I said This means war and the next thing I know I'm in a uniform and in Vietnam. *Vietnam!* ... how the hell did I get there? ... the last thing I can remember saying is This means war and there I was surrounded by artillery fire not from the North Vietnamese but from the fucking lieutenants the generals they didn't know what the fuck they were doing. The soldiers didn't know what they were there for who they were fighting ... bombs were exploding all around us ... I was in the trenches and some guy next to me said Gordon is that a fetal position? and I would turn and look at the body next to me huddled in the mud and say Ha ha ha yes that's a fetal position and we'd take our field glasses and look through them into the fires and see men crossing the fields smoking joints. I'd yell out Hey! are you one of us? and one guy ate his joint and said Yeah now I am ... ha ha ha ... so now the line moves from North America all the half way around the world to Southeast Asia and then they send me back home and I end up over in Berkeley . . . I was in a house living with some friends of my mother's and that's when Mrs. Robinson shows up out of nowhere just materializes out of the air . . . she was this black woman and do you know what she said to me one time? She said You want everything don't you? ha ha ha . . . that bitch here I was on food stamps not a penny to my name and she tells me You want everything well she didn't last long . . . when that creature appeared in the corner of the ceiling one day waving its arms and saying I am god reincarnated Mrs. Robinson took one look at it and ran screaming from the house . . . it said I am god reincarnated . . . I'm a Jehovah's Witness . . . so the line of travel comes from Vietnam to Berkeley . . . now I'm here in San Francisco and planning to go to a logging mill up in Portland for a couple of months . . . but see? that's what their plan is. They want me to go north because that's where the reincarnation process starts . . . see my father was reincarnated into Patrick the guy who lives downstairs. Patrick's eyes are my father's eyes . . . me I don't know exactly where I fit into their plans. I'm sure it's my mother's doing though . . . I should go back and see her and ask her questions and hold a fucking rifle to her head and if she don't give me the right answers I'll blow that bitch's head off . . .

Twenty-Year-Old Woman
in Times Square

NEW YORK CITY

Hey man ... I don't know what to do ... I'm feelin real sick ... last night I got picked up by this trick over on Eighth Avenue at about two in the mornin ... we got a room in this hotel over on Forty-third and got upstairs and he was talkin okay ... ya know I didn't think anything was wrong with him ... so we get into bed and we start makin it and all of a sudden I see this knife and he starts mumblin all this shit and starts cuttin me ... I screamed as loud as I could but like I was in shock ... luckily the man workin the desk the next floor down heard me ... my fuckin arms were just slit up and the door flies open and the manager takes this fuckin guy by the ass and the hair and throws him down the whole flight of stairs ... the fuckin guy ran out into the street naked and disappeared ... look at this ... I fuckin wrapped them up but they haven't stopped bleedin ... ah shit I'm afraid to go to the fuckin hospital cause I think they'll arrest me ... someone gave me these penicillins ... I been takin them so it doesn't get infected but I don't know man ... I feel sick in my stomach ... it's almost fuckin Christmas and I'm supposed to go to Chicago and see my little kids . . . I can't let them see me like this man . . . I'm a fuckin mess . . . this is it man . . . I ain't workin this fuckin city no more . . . I'm gonna take a bus down south . . . away from all these fuckin pimps and screwballs . . . fuck this man . . . I'm goin down south . . .

Kentucky Trucker
in the Rocky Mountains

COLORADO

I make this trip a lot . . . I can pretty much choose my route as far as direction. I'm in between jobs right now I get tired of working so I lay off for a couple of weeks. Usually I hole up in a motel with some woman and a couple bottles of whiskey and burn it all off . . . you can meet some great women driving throughout this country at these truck stops. I picked up this one girl . . . boy was she a wild one. We were cutting along towards Chio and she kept talking like she was rounded up on mollies or some shit then she says to me: How do you know I ain't plannin on pullin out a knife or somethin and killin you for your money? So I eased this pistol I got in my boot out and waved it under her nose. I said: I've been itching to try this out. I got eight hundred dollars in my left ass pocket so when you have the mind to try it you better do the job right. She started giggling and acting like a baby. I almost dumped her off right there on the highway but we kept on and when we reached Columbus we pulled over into a motel and got us a room and had a wild weekend . . . we didn't leave that room except to eat a meal or two . . . she

was like a bobcat in bed, scratching and screaming and giggling the whole time and she didn't touch that fuckin money
or that gun . . . she was alright. See it's the ones who don't
say a word that are really crazy . . . if you're baked upstairs
you don't say a word, you just pull that knife or gun or whatever and use it . . . There ain't no reason to talk about it if
you've got something like that on your mind . . .

There was this one girl I picked last year out in Arizona
. . . real pretty and young . . . so I gave her a ride and we
were about four miles down the interstate when she rips open
her blouse. She doesn't even unbutton it she just rips it open
and messes up her hair and turns to me and says: Look buddy,
you give me fifty bucks right now or I'll start screamin rape.
I said: Holy shit! to myself and reached over and smacked
her as hard as I could and pulled over to the side of the road
and smacked her again and I told her: You go ahead and
scream rape. I'm gonna kick the shit outta you. She started
crying and saying: No no I'm sorry just let me out. I ain't gonna
pull nothing. I'm sorry. So I opened the door and pushed
her out and closed the door and took off. I'll never let anybody pull that shit with me.

Woman in Chinese-American Coffee Shop

SAN FRANCISCO

Oh man when I was in the joint nothin happened . . . I didn't get sick or nothin like I was scared I would . . . I was snortin and shit before I went in . . . and I'm thinkin Oh shit this habit's gonna come up on me cause I was doin ten bags by then . . . but the stuff I was snortin inside kept me goin the whole time I was there . . . I'll tell ya though . . . my lawyer knows just where I am . . . ya know man . . . he can get me for breakin parole any time he wants . . . he just gotta pick up the telephone and have the police pick me up . . . he knows where I live but he don't want to do that cause he knows I'm comin down here for the program every day for the first two years and I ain't been a problem . . . but I almost got picked up last week cause I was doin that shit where I'd let some guy proposition me and then I'd say: Yeah man twenty dollars and I'd take the money off the guy and the first chance I had I would split. Well this guy went and called the police on me man. I couldn't believe it and these two officers grabbed me and asked the guy what I did and the guy said: She took twenty dollars off me and tried to run away, and the cop said: Well how did she get twenty dollars offa you? and the guy says: Well I thought she was a prostitute, and the cop says: Well Miss, you got this guy's twenty bucks? I had forty dollars stuck down the back of my pants so I pulled it out and said: Hey man. I got a ten and two fives in one hand and a twenty in the other. Now you tell me which one is yours and I'll give it back like do you know the serial numbers man? And the guy says: I handed you the ten and two fives so the cop says: Give em back to him . . . so I don't want no trouble so I hand the money back to the guy and the cops take this man to the side and say to him: Now do you want to press charges against this woman? and the guy says: No no. I don't want to press any charges, and the cops say to him: You sure man? and the guy says: Yeah I'm sure I don't wanna press charges. So the cop says: Okay now we're gonna read you your constitutional rights you're under arrest for propositioning this lady. Wow man I couldn't believe it. Ya see the cops didn't let this guy know that they'd arrest him if he didn't press charges cause then that would mean he was wrong if he didn't . . . shit . . . I told the cops that I wouldn't press charges. I said: Hell no man . . . I got enough things to take care of . . . I got a kid comin and another one at home so I can't afford any trouble with goin to court . . . ya know?

Man in Portland
Movie Theater

OREGON

When I was little I used to come to this movie house every chance I got . . . I'd sneak in through the alley . . . I'd tap on the door real soft until one of the people sitting here got up and opened it up for me. Sometimes I'd see the same movie fifteen times . . . the fun of it was hanging out in the balcony with popcorn and ice cream and watching all the goings-on around me in the seats. One time I was hanging out for the late show I was about thirteen years old and I had been to bed with a few guys but I never slept with a girl . . . I had been wanting to for a long time but I was never good on the rap like most of my friends . . . so this one night I was sitting and watching this monster movie some old Dracula film with British actors and I heard someone coming down the aisleway. It was pretty dark up there but I could see it was a woman. She was big not fat but something like six feet tall slightly heavy with big legs she had a huge bustline and she was wearing shocking pink hot pants . . . what a vision . . . every head in the balcony turned. She had these bright red painted lips and she was carrying a little black bag. I watched her enter the line of seats I was in and my heart almost fell out when she sat down a chair away from me . . . there weren't too many people in the balcony that night so she could have chosen a number of other places to sit down in order to be alone so I didn't know what to make of it . . . my mind was racing . . . all these fuckin fantasies . . . I turned back to the screen and kinda let my popcorn drop down to the floor cause it seemed childish to be chewing on popcorn. I was afraid she might see it and get turned off . . . I didn't really know what she was thinking but I was hoping for the best. I kept watch out of the corner of my eye for the longest while and finally let my hand kinda drift down onto the seat between us . . . I let it sit there after a couple of seconds she let hers drift down and slowly covered my hand with hers . . . my heart was racing! I got really red but I was glad it was dark so she couldn't see that. We kinda played with each other's hands and after a few minutes she got up and went back upstairs to the main aisle and disappeared. I wanted to follow her but I was too self-conscious with all those people watching from the other seats . . . my legs were like rubber . . . I watched the film for a few more minutes and then the woman came back down the stairs . . . she was carrying a cola and she came back into my aisle and sat down right next to me . . . in a few seconds she found my hand again and placed it across her breasts. I got a big hard-on and played with her tits for a while. Then I slipped my hands under her blouse and rubbed on her nipples . . . after about fifteen minutes I leaned over and asked her if I could go home with her . . . I was living at home with my parents and there was no way I could bring her there . . . she said her lover lived at home with her but if I wanted to make it with her we could do it down the back stairs of the movie house, it was a staircase hardly anyone used. I was delirious I said yes and we got up and climbed the stairs to the main aisle. I was aware of the guys in the balcony watching us but I was too excited to care. I mean it meant so much to me that in a few minutes I wasn't gonna be a virgin anymore so we went down the back staircase which wasn't lit too well and she took my cock out of my pants and leaning against the wall she pulled down her pants she had her stomach flat against the wall which kinda struck me as weird but I figured she wanted me to enter somehow from behind . . . she took hold of my cock and guided it into her ass . . . I didn't want to fuck her in the ass so I pulled back and tried to get it under her and she moved away . . . all this time I was holding on to her breasts and so then I let my hands go down to her cunt so she would get the message that that's what I wanted . . . when my hands got down near her crotch she gave a wild jump and moved away from me . . . then she stepped back to where she was standing before and took my cock and guided it to her ass this time after placing both of my hands back on her breasts . . . I don't know what it was but something made me suspicious . . . she wouldn't let me go near her crotch with my hands so I started playing with her breasts again and at the same time I moved back slowly so that in order to get my cock into her ass she would have to move away from the wall. When she did this and was far enough away from the wall to give me room I quick slipped my hands down to her crotch and sure enough there was a cock and balls there. The guy turned around with this look of terror on his face . . . his mouth fell open and he looked like he was afraid I was going to beat him up . . . I was upset . . . it was like some kind of fantasy that had slowly started coming true and then it was suddenly exploded. I just said: Oh fuck! and pushed him away. I pulled up my pants and rushed down the stairs and out into the street . . . I felt like crying but I just ran all the way home . . .

Fourteen-Year-Old Runaway Girl

WOODSTOCK

think I need some kind of care . . . not mental care ya know but medical care because I think my heart's bad . . . I gotta bad heart I get heart attacks all the time . . . I just keep movin around. Ya know what I'm doing? I'm lookin for Bob Dylan. I think he's in California or maybe he's back in New York City . . . but I figure I gotta be in control of myself before I meet him . . . I don't want him to say: Hey look, you're just a little kid, real young . . . ya gotta grow up.

I only talk with guys that got hook noses, with noses like Bob Dylan's. I find I can usually get along with them . . . like they're more sensitive . . . I talk to sensitive guys cause they're good for me . . . they know what I'm talkin about . . . they do things for me ya know? I sometimes talk with guys with other kinds of noses, sensitive noses . . . like yours . . .

I was in a program for a while, in a hospital. They taught me to see myself . . . let myself come through . . . that's why I'm much nicer than last year. Last year I was angry but that was because people would come up and make faces at me . . .

people play a lot of games ya know? At the hospital I went through a lot of stuff . . . sometimes I'd get real angry . . . I wouldn't get violent, I'm not a violent person but I'd get physical ya know? like I'd hit somebody but I knew what I was doing . . . it was like a game . . . I'd say to myself: I'll hit that person and then I'll say I'm sorry . . . but the program was good . . . we had to be on detroxin or destroxan or something like that . . . a shot every two weeks . . . not a shot that hurt . . . and I'd feel good . . .

I don't hitchhike, I'll hitchhike only if I know the place I'm going . . . like if I was goin to Jersey I'd hitchhike cause I know Jersey . . . but I meet strange guys on the road. One time I was hitchin in Kansas and this big fat guy picked me up . . . we were drivin along and all of a sudden he reached over and grabbed my arm. I said: Oh shit and tried to jump out of the car but he wouldn't let me so I quick tore my arm away and got the door opened and jumped out. He yelled out at me: *Don't you get back in this car girlie.*

I gotta get some ID so I can go to work but I don't remember what hospital I was born in and my mother died and my father retired and is somewhere in Florida and I can't get the name of the hospital . . . I figure maybe I should go back to the program . . . that's the best thing for me cause my image of myself is totally shattered . . . I might have pneumonia . . . I got this terrible cough and I'm allergic to sugar . . . I wanna get me a guitar and a harmonica once I start workin . . . then I can practice and get good at it . . . and I'll go down to the Village around Bleecker Street and find me some folkies and we'll all live together and get the revolution started again . . .

Young Guy Hanging Out
on Market Street

SAN FRANCISCO

I used to hustle with a buddy but things got bad between us . . . it was hard cause we were good friends for a long time before we hustled together and we just couldn't get it on with a guy in front of each other so some guy would pick us up, see we'd help each other out by tellin guys that we wouldn't go with them without each other, some guys dug the idea of two kids but when we'd get up to their place we'd end up not wantin to go down on the guy or whatever while the other was watchin. That caused a lot of hassles and sometimes it'd almost keep us from gettin paid. The last time me and my friend hustled together some spade approached my friend and told him that there was a guy waitin in the parking lot around the corner who was interested in makin it with him. My friend said he wouldn't do it without me comin along, so the spade checked it out with the guy and the guy said okay. We walked around the corner and into the parking lot and there was this black limo sittin there. This young couple got out of the limo and stood there watchin us as we walked up . . . it was weird . . . I can remember the girl was real beau-

tiful and she gave me this funny look with these sad eyes, I
mean we were pretty young, only about thirteen or fourteen,
so this fat guy inside the limo told us to get in and we did.
He had this color TV and a pink phone in the backseat of the
car and a driver with a uniform. So we agreed that he'd pay
us fifty bucks each and then we drove to this fancy apartment building. The guy lived on the thirtieth floor . . . he told
us he was with the Mafia. When we got inside his apartment
he showed us a bunch of San Francisco Police badges and a
German Luger. It was a pretty gun, had a clip with seven
copper-tip bullets in it . . . my friend picked up the gun and
aimed it right between my eyes and I almost kicked the shit
out of him for it . . . thank god the fuckin gun wasn't loaded
. . . so this guy starts suckin us off and then after a while he
sees we ain't gonna do anything in front of each other so he
takes my friend into the other room. After a few minutes my
friend came out and tells me the guy wants me to go in. Well
I got in the room and I lay out on the bed and the guy flips
me over and tries to stick it in me . . . it was killin me . . . he's
breathin in my ear like a sick hog goin: I'll give ya another
twenty-five bucks if ya let me. I couldn't get him off me he
weighed too much and he kept trying to stick it in . . . finally
I twisted over and the two of us fell off the bed on the floor
like a fucking earthquake boom! so the guy gave us our money
and told us to get out . . . we split and after that I stopped
hustlin with my friend . . .

A couple of times we tried to do some muggin to get some
money but we were really bad at it, we didn't have the guts
for it. One night we stayed up all night walkin around the
fuckin city tryin to find an easy mark. Around four in the
morning we spied some guy with a suit walkin about three
blocks away and we figured we would run as fast as we could

and slam into him, knock him down and grab his wallet and run. So we started runnin and we get up right behind the guy and he must've heard us cause he turned around and we saw that he was just an old bum wearin some suit that was too big for him and we burst out laughin right there . . . it was awful. Another guy we met was real drunk and we started talkin to him tryin to get invited up to his place for a drink. We figured we'd tie him up and take whatever was in the place and fence it. So we wandered round with the guy for three hours makin friends with him. At one point he gave my friend five bucks to go get him a pack of cigarettes at the all-night coffee shop. My friend ran down and got the cigarettes and while he was gone the guy started tellin me how he was wounded in World War II and how he laid up in the hospital for a year and a half and then he started crying and tellin me about how his father died in World War I and how he still missed him after fifty-something years. I almost started crying cause it made me think of my father . . . I mean the guy really reminded me of how my father was when he got drunk. Well my friend came runnin up with the cigarettes and the guy was thankful for the favor. He invited us back to his place for food or somethin. My friend said yeah yeah but I told the guy no we had to get goin and maybe some other time. My friend got pissed off at me and after the guy split I tried to explain to him why I couldn't go through with it . . . he thought I was off my rocker . . .

Man in Mickey's
Dining Car 2:30 A.M.

ST. PAUL

I've been living here a few weeks and it's starting to get a little hot for me . . . I've written myself out of several states in the last six years . . . Florida would love to get a hold of me I'm sure . . . see I was working for a bank seven years ago. I worked in the section that dealt with the papers and accounts of persons deceased. I was cashing checks against the accounts of this doctor who had dropped dead and whose money was tied up pending the outcome of some wills he'd left behind. I finally got snagged and did a little time in Elmira for it . . . it was easy for me to go through it . . . if you got a little money on the outside you can get a lot of shit . . . steaks, drugs, even women if you pay enough . . . but I ain't that interested in women . . . too much time in prisons changed all that. I've been mostly going with young boys from every meat market between L.A. and New York City . . . lots of cute kids out there. I got four sets of checkbooks from dead doctors and a load of ID and some sweet fuckin smiles that pay my way through every state. See that kid over there he's into smack pretty bad. I've known him since I got here and he's hustling down by the terminal just about every night . . . sweet kid, lemme tell ya. I did something that I ain't proud of . . . don't know why I did it and it's left me with a bad taste about myself . . . I can't look the kid in the face no more. See I've wanted to fuck the kid since I met him but he's always refused and there was no way I could get him to turn over in bed. Two nights ago he came up to my hotel room pretty sick . . . he said he had to get some money fast did I wanna trick with him. It was awful he was getting the sweats already and in pain. I told him: How bad do you need the money? bad enough to turn over? He started crying but he turned over and I went ahead and fucked him . . . gave him thirty extra cause I felt so fuckin guilty afterwards. I really don't know what to say . . . I don't know why I did it to him . . . he hasn't said a word to me since then and I figure it's about time I split from here . . . maybe head back to New York. There's some halfway houses I can work in keep a low profile for a while anyway . . .

Young Boy in
Times Square 4:00 A.M.

NEW YORK CITY

I t's okay down here . . . I got lots of friends lots of people
watchin out for me . . . a couple of prostitutes are like my
second parents . . . they give me money for coffee or cigarettes when things are tight . . . I let em know when I see the
vans comin around . . . I tell ya I learned more down here
about real people in a year than the last seven years in school.
Tell me what the fuck Lewis and Clark would do if they sailed
down the Hudson and got off on Forty-second Street and they
didn't have no money to get somethin to eat . . . I could hook
em up with a guy who'd put both of em in soft fuck films in
a second . . . ha ha . . . no no, really I do okay down here . . .
there's a weirdo once in a while but most of the guys are
nice . . . ya learn to pick em out by the way they move . . . if
a man's crazy you can pick it up in his eyes in a second.
There's other ways to pick up money besides hustlin the
Square . . . by Saturday afternoon business is bad . . . most of
the payin johns have got some kid for the weekend and there's
not too much goin on . . . there's this crazy kid I know he's
been showin me a lot of shit . . . he took me out to Coney

Island and hipped me to kickin clothes . . . that's when ya
get two kids like me and him and ya take off your shirts just
like any normal kids on a beach and when it's crowded ya
run down the beach chasin each other and every once in a
while ya stop and throw each other around in the sand and
all ya gotta do is keep a smile on your face and laugh a lot
like you're just two kids havin fun . . . then ya get over by a
blanket where there's some pairs of pants folded up and if
no one's watchin close ya chase each other past the blanket
and kick the pair of pants in front of you . . . ya just keep
shouting and laughin and kickin the fuckin pants down the
beach till ya get a ways away and then ya fall down like you're
out of breath. If no one comes screamin down at ya for kickin
their pants around ya go through the pockets and take whatever money's there . . . we did this for a whole summer on
the weekends . . . I finally stopped doin it though cause the
last time I did it see usually I'd let my friend kick the pants
and we'd split it fifty-fifty but he got tired of it and said if I
didn't kick for a while he'd give me a smaller cut so I started
kickin and about the seventh time I kicked we got far down
on the beach and I reached into the pants for the wallet. It
was thick like there was a lot of money and when I opened
it my eyes almost took a vacation there was this fuckin gold
detective badge hooked inside it . . . I gave it up then and
there. This guy hipped me to a lot of other things too. We'd
ride dumbwaiters up and down these old buildings in Brooklyn from the roof and kick in doors and pick up some cash.
Sometimes we'd raid the refrigerator if there was anything
worthwhile in there. Lemme tell ya this guy is crazy though
. . . a couple of weeks ago he walked into this butcher shop
downtown the owners were busy in the back makin repairs
and he walked over and picked the key to the register off
the wall and opened the cash drawer. There was about three
hundred bucks inside. He stuffed it into a shopping bag and

walked out. We bought a couple of tubes of glue and a pair of socks and split to Jersey for the day. We went to this amusement park and sniffed behind the beauty show stage and walked around in the freak show for a while. We saw this two-headed turtle in a jar of alcohol and a load of pictures of women with small bodies growin out of their bellies. We ate too much food and then my friend got the idea that we should ride the octopus and sniff while it's going around so we went up and this fuckin machine is goin up and down and spinnin around every once in a while. I started getting sick from the glue. They put this onion or garlic oil in it now so that ya get sick if ya sniff it. So I started getting ready to heave and I yelled down to these two guys runnin the machine: Whoa let me off I'm gonna be sick and these fuckin guys think it's funny. They start pointin at me and laughin like it's a big joke so I start chuckin and I hold it in till we're stopped right over the guys runnin the ride. We're spinnin and I let go . . . it was like a fuckin April shower all over em . . . well they stopped the fuckin ride fast and when I got off I could hardly walk and these two guys are screamin at me: Why the hell you go on ride if you sick! . . . ha ha . . . they were covered, man . . .

. . . last night was the first time I ever saw a guy and a girl fuck . . . I was in the Comet Hotel over on Forty-fifth Street and this guy brought me up there and asked special for room number seven . . . he must've known what the room was like cause after we got in there he had me take off my clothes and then he pulled up a chair to the door that separates our room from the next room. It's like a double room for families but they keep the door locked when only one room's being rented. So there's this big crack in the door and when the guy shut out the lights you could look into the next room without being noticed. So he had me wait till someone rented out the next room and then he had me watch what was goin on while he went down on me . . . it was crazy . . . this prostitute I remember from in front of the Port Authority walked in with this Spanish guy and they threw off their clothes and the guy hops on the bed and this girl jumped on top of him and the two of them went at it, changin positions every couple of seconds until he shot, then she got up and put her leg up on the bed and took a wipe at herself with a towel and they got dressed again. The whole thing took two minutes and when she turned around to get into her dress I could see this huge area of her chest and stomach all scarred up . . . fresh scars with stitches in em . . . I almost puked . . . the guy I was with gave me a lot to make up for it but it flipped me out . . . it made me feel really funny watchin them . . .

Young Runner

Hanging Out by the River

THE BRONX

know this guy who deals amyl nitrite. A friend of his, this chemist, makes it pure, not like that shit they sell over at candy stores, so this guy I know sells it for him. Last night we were out running along the river when he says: Look I gotta stop by some guy's house to drop off some amyl ya wanna come? So I said: Yeah so we took a run over to this house over in the middle of the neighborhood, this old place built around the 1800s. We ring the bell and this heavyset priest opens the door. He's wearing these thick glasses and he's got a funny look on his face like maybe I shouldn't be there. Then he invites us in and starts apologizing for this mess in the hallway. It was a huge load of Louis the XIV antiques obviously worth a shitload of money. So we go down the front hall and this ratty little dog jumps out at us. It was like a poodle but fat as a watermelon. It started shrieking and gurgling and running around in circles and the priest takes us into this living room filled with tons of porcelain and crystal and brass and this little dog follows us in jumping into the air doing little pirouettes and licking us all over our bare legs and fingers . . . it was disgusting . . . and we're sitting there and my friend and this priest are shooting the breeze when this cellar door opens and this other priest comes up with another dog. This dog was about as big as me and fuckin ugly and when it walked over to me and stared at me for a few minutes without moving I felt obliged to give it a pat cause the two priests were watching me. Then this one priest says: Oh please please don't pet the dog she's really quite old and paranoid. She may bite. Man, what a fuckin relief. So my friend gives these two priests a couple of bottles of amyl and they start talking about their drug experiences. The priest with the glasses turns to me and says: Now I hope this doesn't shock you. I said: Oh no, and he goes on about how he tried this THC that a student gave him and it was: Ab-so-lute-ly marvelous and how he copped twenty tabs of it cause: It has all the effects of marijuana without the fuss and mess. It was like a fuckin commercial. The other priest didn't say anything but: Um ah hum. And this heavy guy kept talking about doing acid and how he was worried he'd have a flashback while he was working. Then he got into talking about guys he's been to bed with, how this guy named Stone from Coney Island had a big cock and how this other guy from the Village had a bigger cock and how this guy he met on vacation in Puerto Rico knew how to fuck best of all and how he had thoughts about this student who was hung like an ox . . . I don't know man . . . it just sounded so fuckin lonesome . . .

Young Woman in Coffee Shop
on the Lower East Side

NEW YORK CITY

Sometimes when I'm walking through the streets I want my fingernails to grow long and hard so I can make scratches in the concrete or make grooves in the sidewalk or scratch windows or by concentrating real hard make all the windows shatter and rain down on the street or make cigarette smoke go back into cigarettes like a film running backwards or make the streets crack open like earthquakes like huge crevices split open in the surface of the asphalt. Sometimes I think by staring hard enough I can make the sky turn into a storm, make dark clouds suddenly twist around and send rain and lightning over the rooftops. Sometimes if I'm feeling frustrated and men hassle me on the street I wish I could raise my hand and suddenly dimes would be welded on their eyeballs so they couldn't see where they were going. And when guys on the street make kiss noises at me I wish I could make their dicks wither and drop off.

Sometime I'd like to make a film of a woman murdering someone in which she stabs the person butchers and dismembers him rips his stomach open and at the end of this she sits down in the midst of all this, her clothes and hands and face all covered in blood and she starts crying . . .

Guy in Car on
Wall Street at Midnight

NEW YORK CITY

'll never go to Texas again swear to ya, I won't ever go there again. Last time I was there see, I met this guy in a bar in Arizona where I was growin up and he invited me to visit him in Dallas. I was young and didn't let my parents know I was goin. I just packed a small overnight bag with some clothes and I took a flight there and met up with this guy and it was during the day so he took me for a walk on the grounds of this psychiatric hospital that he worked in and he said: Not only do I work here but I once lived here . . . I was a patient, and I remember laughing nervously and saying: Oh yeah, therapy does anyone a world of good. You probably feel better now. And then we went to his apartment sitting in his bedroom and he's gettin depressed and starts talking about killing himself and says it'll be easy to take me with him and he says he's got this gun in the car and I'm thinking oh my god my parents don't even know I'm here and if he kills himself the police will come and what would my parents say when they found out and then he says I don't need to go down to the car I got knives in the kitchen and he rushes in and pulls open a drawer and I followed right behind him and he pulls out this fuckin meat cleaver and I'm wrestling with him over the meat cleaver and this was a big guy and I was pretty young and I wrestle the cleaver out of his hand after banging all around the kitchen and I pull open the door of the apartment and throw the thing as far as I could but he turns around and runs back into the kitchen and I start running like hell and knock over the television set and a table and some chairs and there's this guy sleeping on the couch some next-door neighbor had asked if a guest who was visiting him could sleep on this guy's couch and I ran through the room and threw open the door and started screaming like hell and he woke up and I was screaming at him telling him what was happening and he was sitting there like: Uh. He couldn't believe it and suddenly the guy comes out of the kitchen. He just snapped out of it and he was saying: Alright, alright. Be calm I'm okay now. And I grabbed my bag and took the next flight back . . .

Boy in Coffee Shop
on Third Avenue

NEW YORK CITY

used to hustle over in the Square but I don't no more . . . too many creeps wackos loonies. I hustled just about every night runnin tricks for anything between ten and twenty-five bucks. I'd save a lot of it up for the weekend when a friend of mine, this guy who lived out in Queens who I met in summer camp, we'd hang out together and do crazy stuff. I'd save my money and that way we'd have a lot to blow when we got together. I mean he was into hustlin too but rather than waste all weekend gettin up the bucks for a good time I'd hustle during the week and give him half when he came over. The last time I hustled the Square I had about fifty bucks in my shoe . . . it'd been a fucked up night and I was trying to get twenty more and then I was gonna call it quits. This was on a Friday night and my friend was gonna come over the next morning. So it's about 10:30 and I ain't found no one for about two hours, heat must have been on, I don't know, so anyway I'm standin lookin in this sporting goods store window and I see this guy about thirty years old checkin me out from the corner of his eye. I'd seen him around every now and then, not too often but I'd seen him around so we got to talkin and I told him that I wanted twenty bucks and he said yeah okay and we decided to go down to Forty-first Street around Tenth or Eleventh Avenue so we could save him the money for a room. That's where they park some city buses that they ain't usin . . . so we get down there and on the way down we pass the train lines and he says: Let's squeeze through the fence and do it in there. So I followed him in and he tells me to go down on him. Here we are standin on this two-foot ledge about thirty feet above the tracks and rocks and I go down on him but he can't seem to get it up. A couple of cars come down and their headlights almost picked us out so he says: Fuck this, let's go over to the buses. So we go behind this long line of buses and he tells me to go down on him again and as I'm doin this he still doesn't get a hard-on and I start wondering if something's wrong when all of a sudden I hear this voice come from him . . . it was real strange like he was crazy . . . he says: Hey kid get up slow now. I'm a vice cop and you're under arrest. I stood up and almost passed out. I started cryin and he goes: Okay give me all your money, all of it. I tell him I only have about seventy cents, like I don't tell him about the fifty in my shoe and he says: Look if I gotta search ya and I find any more than this I'm gonna kill ya. So I said: Hey man this is all I got. That's why I was out there hustlin tonight. So then he says: Oh yeah? What about in your shoes, got any money in there? I say no and he says: Well take them off then. So I reached for the shoe that didn't have the money in it and just as I got it untied he says: Forget it. Then he says: Ya know you can go to reform school for this. I can take you in and call your parents and bring you through family court. I just kept shakin and then he says: Drop your pants and turn around. I did it and he grabbed me and tried to shove his cock up my ass. It hurt really bad so I kept pullin away and finally he reached in his jacket and pulled out this big knife . . . that's when I knew the fuckin guy wasn't a cop . . . so I stopped strugglin and he came quick and then told me to pull up my pants. When I did he grabbed me by the shoulder and started walkin me towards the river. I was shittin bricks at this point cause I knew if he planned to let me go he would've by now cause there was nobody around but he had other plans and we walked down to Eleventh and then towards Twelfth and this guy didn't say nothin the whole way just starin straight ahead with his hand on my shoulder. Then everything happened so fast. This city bus pulled up out of nowhere about forty yards away and stopped at the curb. I could see it was empty except for the driver who was sittin there writin in his pad. So I turned real quick and gave this guy a shove and ran like hell towards the bus screamin at the top of my lungs. The guy chased me a couple of yards then turned and ran in the other direction. I stopped and turned around and screamed: *You ain't no fuckin cop, ya bastard!* and started runnin again only past the bus. The driver was sittin there with his mouth open wonderin what the fuck was goin on. I circled the block and ran up Fortieth Street towards Eighth Avenue and just as I turned the corner of Ninth Avenue I almost ran smack into the fuckin phony cop. He didn't see me but he was comin my way at a fast walk and I dove down between two parked cars and let him pass before I got up and continued runnin uptown. That whole thing left me with a weird feelin . . . I've only been close to death two times in my life and each time it left me feelin kinda weak . . . like not scared or crazy or anything . . . it's just that ya get this feeling like: Man, it's that easy, it's like you can die that fast or simple or whatever and you don't feel no wiser or you don't feel like you got a new start on living . . . it just amazes you that your time can come up just like that before you can even decide to go straight and clean or change your fuckin socks or say good-bye to your friends . . . like after I got away I sat down on a street corner near my house and waited for the fuckin tears to come but all I could do was shake my head and decide I'd never go down to that Square again . . .

Young Boy in
Bus Station Coffee Shop

DENVER

Yeah . . . I almost got killed when I was going cross country . . . but I guess everybody comes close to death at least once if they make that kind of distance. I was in Las Vegas . . . man Las Vegas was beautiful . . . well I was hanging out at this apartment with two roommates. We were all working at different hours. One of the roommates owned a motorcycle and one day when he was at work my other roommate turned to me and said: Hey let's take a ride on the motorcycle. He didn't have a license or nothing but I said: Okay and we split going around the roads in and out of town and all of a sudden we passed this fuckin cop car. We kept going and this cop car circles around and starts following us. We turned down one street and then another and the fuckin cop was still following us. Finally he puts on his flashing lights and gave a few blasts at his siren so we pulled over to the side of the road down at the bottom of a hill near a fork. The cop pulls to the side and starts getting out of the car and right across the road is this path that cuts through a forest to another highway so my roommate driving the motorcycle waits till the cop is a few yards away and then guns the fuckin bike and cuts across the road onto the path. The cop made this big scramble to get back to his car and he goes blowing out in the dust to chase us. We were heading through to the other highway and we made it and started heading further away from town. The cop car was coming up behind us pretty fast with the siren screaming he was weaving in and out of traffic and so were we. We finally cut to the side of the road to get past all the slow cars and the cop saw what was happening and did the same. Now we're really going fast as hell and getting further and further away from town . . . we kept cutting down side roads and finally we turned down this one street and it was a dead end . . . there was nothing in front of us but the whole goddamn desert so we said: Oh shit! and we hear the cop car racing down behind us. We had been traveling up to eighty miles per hour with this cop behind us. So my friend guns the motor again and we cut out into the desert. We were going about twenty-five miles per hour brrooommmm up and down these slopes and dunes and hills with this fucking cop still behind us and we got pretty far out but then we went up the side of this slope and it turned out to be a small cliff on the other side and the bike dropped off and we went through the air and slammed into the sand at the bottom. I had the wind knocked out of me and I could hear the cop coming so I stood up and turned around with my hands in the air waiting for him to come over the rise and get me. I figured there was nowhere else we could go because the bike was smashed up from the fall and this cop comes running over the slope towards me and he drops to his knees in a crouching position and aims his gun and shouts: Halt you sonuvabitch! Halt! and I turn around and there's my roommate running commando style across the fuckin desert dodging back and forth. I couldn't fuckin believe it. So the cop handcuffs me and I'm lying there on my side in the sand

and he radios for reinforcements. About twenty minutes later two squad cars show up and these big beefy bastards pull out a bunch of dogs. They were out there about two hours sniffing around but they never got the guy. I don't know how the hell he got away. So they took me back to town and threw me in jail. I was in there for three days under the charge of grand larceny resisting arrest and some other shit . . . but let me tell you it was alright in that jail . . . I just slept and ate . . . I mean I would rather have not been there but the guys in the cell block were right guys. We would write these notes on small pieces of paper and shove them through the slots in the doors and wiggle them around to try and get the guard's attention in the early morning when they walked through the cell block. You know, notes like: HEY I'M INNOCENT or PLEASE CALL THIS NUMBER FOR ME. After the day they finally let me make a phone call they took me into this empty room with bars over everything and they got this fuckin ugly cop leaning back in a chair against the wall smoking a pipe and a radio was playing. I called my other roommate and he came down to convince them that the bike was his and that I didn't steal it. The cops tried to get me to say who it was who was driving the bike but I kept telling them that I didn't know, that I knew he knew my roommate but that I had never seen him before in my life. Two days later I was taken to court and they let me off . . .

Young Man in
Silver Dollar Restaurant

NEW YORK CITY

One night I was down by the Hudson River around the parking lot where out-of-towners cruise in their cars and I was walkin around checkin out the river and the people. I walked to the end of the lot where there's not too many cars and this voice says hello and I turn and there's this handsome guy sittin in his car with the motor going so I walk over and lean on the door and talk to him for a while. He was pretty cool, I mean friendly and handsome . . . I checked out his body his arms and chest were really nice and I glanced down at his crotch but it was in the shadows. After a while he asked me to get in the car and go for a ride. We went up the Hudson to a place along the river in the Twenties or Thirties where there's this old railroad track that ends suddenly at the river's edge. It was a hot night and the windows were open and he pulls out some reefer and we were smokin and talkin for a while. At some point his hand slid over onto my leg and I was feelin good so I reached over and put my palm on his chest and rubbed it slow, moving down towards his crotch. When my hand reached his legs it just passed through the air . . . I mean my hand suddenly went into nothingness . . . you know that moment when your brain is given information that's almost too much for it to deal with, like something so unexpected that it can't be broken down right away . . . I stopped for a second and this guy's still rubbing around my leg and I decided that I was just going to ignore the fact that he had no legs and at some point he reached over me and hit this lever on the bottom of my seat and it made the seat fly back so I was parallel to the ground and he does the same to his seat and then lifts himself up on his arms and swings up and over onto me and I close my eyes and move with it. After we had sex he told me he lost his legs in Vietnam, he said he stepped on a minefield two days before he was gonna head home . . . so he's sittin there in this field still conscious with both his legs gone and he sees this helicopter comin to rescue him and it landed right on a mine and blew up . . . three copters one after another blew up trying to rescue him and finally they got him outta there. After tellin me this he suddenly says desperately: I need some hot water right away so I give him directions to my place and he pulls up outside of my house and says: Make it really hot and bring a rag or somethin . . . he seems almost hysterical so I don't question it. I run upstairs boil some water and bring it down in a plastic container. He asks if he can keep it and I say Yeah and he takes off. I go upstairs and my boyfriend comes outta his room and says: What's going on? and I don't know what to say . . .

Night Guard
in a Bookstore

NEW YORK CITY

I wear a watch out of habit not because I need it but I'm always checking what time it is . . . that's what makes this job drag so much . . . I wore a watch for the last forty years . . . had to in the job I had before. I worked in a power company in New Jersey . . . had to check the pumps and water like every minute . . . had to check it against my watch and when it got hot I had to let more water in and check my watch again. When I married my first wife I needed a job and she was working for this company. She tried to get me some work and they said they weren't hiring but then they called up one day asking Would you work in a boiler room? I said sure I'll do the work. Them days it was tough trying to get someone for the boiler room . . . most guys never lasted . . . I worked in there till about 1938. Then I quit after I divorced my first wife . . . I should've stayed cause now they're having a picnic. They got themselves some new hydraulic pumps and modern machines so they hardly do nothing. Had I stayed I'd be an assistant foreman, would've been walking around with a tie and white shirt.

* * *

Then I worked for the Jersey Pacific railroad for seven months
. . . see this bump on my hand? I can pick up something heavy
for a while and it'll raise right back up. Look at it. I could
peel it right off and it'll grow right back . . . can't get rid of
these things ever . . . I got it using these big air machines, we
called them guns, used them to straighten the tracks. They'd
drop lots of stones underneath them. We'd go along the tracks
with guns and you know those big machines they use to break
up the streets outside? well it was those kind of machines
but worse, louder and heavier. We'd follow right along the
tracks and use them to push the track down into the ground
breaking up the rocks till they lay straight. At the end of the
day I'd go home couldn't hear a thing. I'd yell at my wife:
For christsake can't you talk no louder? I couldn't hear a word
she was saying. There we were just married and she had to
yell at me I couldn't hear a word. And boy did she double-
cross me . . . I'll tell you I should've done what I planned to
do the night before the wedding. I was gonna call the whole
thing off. I liked her a lot and we got along fine but then her
family comes down from Pennsylvania a couple of days before the wedding . . . I should've known then it was no good
. . . and as soon as they see me her sister and her mother and
father starts lettin right into me telling me I better do this and
I better do that. Her sister kept saying I was a no-good bum,
why didn't I have a better job. I finally got so sick of it I said:
To hell with all of you the wedding's off and I walked right
out of the room and down the stairs. All of a sudden my wife
was right next to me begging me not to pay her family no
mind. I said Look you and me get along fine but then they
come down and start telling me this and that hell I ain't mar-
rying your family, I want to marry you. Her mother and sister
came running down the stairs saying they were sorry and
everything. So I let up and we got married. Boy was that

woman nice as could be before we got married then all of a sudden she changed . . . started up the same stuff her family did. Let me tell you I told myself after my first wife I'd never marry again but I did and I made a mistake. I'm still married to her but I've been separated for thirty years . . . she wanted to divorce me . . . her lawyer called me up about the papers and all I said was one thing to him and he called her back and said: Forget it I ain't getting myself involved in this thing at all. So I didn't let her get the divorce but I was a fool . . . I should've given it to her when she first wanted it . . . I made my first wife pay for the divorce but my second wife . . . I didn't let her have one . . . I should've when she first wanted it . . .

Boy on the Lower East Side

NEW YORK CITY

I was workin up in Provincetown this summer . . . it was a desperate situation lemme tell ya . . . I was workin as a chambermaid desk clerk short-order cook and waiter. Not only that but sometimes I was handyman cause there were these porch windows that opened out onto the deck and sometimes they would fall out and I had to fix them. I mean they did have a handyman for a while, this 300-pound guy named Bobo who wore Hawaiian shirts and tight shorts. He'd drive around in this '56 Chevy, a real bomb I tell ya, cruisin people on the sly. Anyway he dropped out of sight. I think a hitchhiker did him in cause he was always pickin up hitchhikers and trying to cruise them. One day these cops came in after he hadn't shown up for work for a while and they showed me photos and asked me if I knew him. I said: Yeah I know him. He used to work here but we haven't seen him around. In fact we have a check in the safe for him. The cops said he was missing and they never did find him . . .

Well one weekend I was hangin out at this hotel called the Tortilla Flat with some friends of mine, this girl named Janet

Planet who had a roommate we called Morphine Marie. Janet Planet and I were comin back from this restaurant when we bumped into this guy named Chuck who lived at the Tortilla Flat. He was a drug dealer and into drugs himself and when we found him he was wanderin around goin: Where's my dog I lost my dog but the guy didn't even have a fuckin dog. It turned out he had swallowed ten or more downs. We didn't know how long he had them in him so we started walking him around to keep him from goin to sleep. Finally we got tired of doin that so we took him back to the hotel and put him in his room. We kept watch over him cause he kept turnin over on his stomach to fall asleep . . . we had to keep turnin him on his back cause we were afraid he'd start to puke and maybe drown in it. It was intense cause we had to do this every ten minutes and then right in the middle of all this a friend of Chuck's came burstin into the room with news that the police were plannin a big bust that evening and Chuck's name might be on the list. And I guess a whole lot of other people's names were on the list cause it seemed everybody we knew was packin up and leavin town. The police got wise to the fact that everybody split so they called off the raid. So after we made sure Chuck was okay me and Janet Planet split and go down to the lobby and there's this little five-year-old kid who was the son of Morphine Marie. Here he was with this piece of paper in his hand sittin in the middle of the floor. Morphine Marie had sent him downstairs with this fuckin note after takin a hundred downs. The note said: TAKE CARE OF THIS KID . . . IT'S ALL OVER FOR ME . . . so we quick rushed up to her room and kicked in the door and there was Morphine Marie lyin across the mattress completely out of it. We called the rescue squad and they came and rushed her to the hospital and pumped her stomach. They took away her kid cause she was always abusin him . . . she used to beat him up . . . a nice kid real cute . . .

* * *

So I got back to my hotel and was readin and later in the
evening my roommate this guy named Grace comes in with
this guy named Arnie who was livin off this woman in town
named Annabel who worked for one of the wealthiest people
in the area, some guy who adopted somethin like ten or
eleven kids, even adopted a couple of twenty-five-year-old
brothers. This guy was fucked up cause he used to sleep with
the kids he adopted. So Grace comes in with this guy Arnie
who had all these prison tattoos of snakes and shit up and
down his arms. Arnie was straight and was just interested in
getting a blow job and Grace met him in the street and brought
him up to the room to get it on but when Arnie got there he
ended up bein more interested in me than he was in Grace
. . . so he kept trying to come on to me . . . like I thought he
was kinda interesting but because he wasn't into being mu-
tual in sex I figured Fuck this. Grace got pissed off cause Arnie
was ignorin him so he started in on the wine we had in the
house. After he finished the wine he went downstairs and
broke into the hotel owner's private liquor cabinet and
grabbed a couple of bottles of Scotch and brought them back
up to the room and polished off one bottle and started on
the other. So he ended up pretty drunk and tryin to get Arnie
to go to bed with him but Arnie just ignored him and kept
buggin me. So I got tired of the whole thing and it was pretty
late so I went into my room and lay down on the bed to try
and go to sleep . . . I mean I didn't want this fuckin Arnie to
come near me so here I am tryin to sleep and Arnie gets up
and comes into my room followed by Grace. Everybody in
the fuckin house comes into my room and Grace starts hangin
all over Arnie and Arnie keeps pushin Grace off him and tryin
to talk me into getting it on with him and I'm thinkin: Jesus
Christ I'm tryin to get some sleep so Grace starts gettin rough
and grabbin Arnie and finally Arnie starts hittin him and finally

punches Grace out. So Grace gets up and starts screamin . . . lemme tell ya it wasn't just yellin . . . Grace was screechin at the top of his voice . . . so I turned to Ronald, one of the guys who was adopted by that rich guy Annabel worked for . . . I figured he was the only one who didn't have that much to drink so I turned to him and said: Get rid of him will ya? Now when I said Get rid of him I meant for him to get rid of Grace. I shoulda said: Get rid of her, then Ronald woulda understood, but he thinks I meant get rid of Arnie so what does the jerk do? He goes downstairs to the lobby and calls the police. Now Arnie was on the lam from paroles in Boston and this is all he needs right now. So the fuckin police come and lemme tell ya, my room was a wipeout . . . I had all these fuckin clothes and books strewn all over the chest and floor and hangin out of closets, and all these people in there yellin and screamin and it's dark on top of that. So the police arrive and as soon as they open the door Grace stops screamin and Arnie stops yellin and the whole place goes silent and Ronald says: Look get rid of that guy, and points to Arnie. Luckily all the police do is escort Arnie downstairs and out the door and they let him go without checkin up on him. Right after all this is over fuckin Grace goes into the other room and starts laughin like crazy . . .

Man on Christmas Eve
along the Rainy Hudson River
3:00 A.M.

NEW YORK CITY

I don't know if you can understand this, what you might feel about this but I want to box with you, get the sense of us both in the room boxing gloves tied over our hands our clothes off and naked boxing with each other . . . I don't mean S/M I'm not into giving pain to anyone in that sense . . . I don't want anyone who could be dominated either. I want that sense of resistance and yet simultaneously of submission . . . I want it to be a trade-off of blows. First you punch me in the chest then I'll give you a right to your chin a slam in your chest blow for blow maybe occasionally jerking each other off maybe going down on each other. I want to do this with you but I have to know that the idea would turn you on, you have to have a sense of the eroticism inherent in two men trading punches . . . the line being drawn at defeat . . . see I'm not interested in beating the shit out of you and I'm not interested in being beaten up myself like I can't see either of us being dominated by the other . . . that would break the whole sense of us as men . . . I'm not attracted to these leather guys with S.S. uniforms they're screaming queens anyway I have no desire for uniforms or images of that sort. These guys who are into masochism are under the impression that it's psychically as well as physically gratifying but really all they are doing is warping their psyches because a person cannot be continually dominated without that sense invading and overpowering his entire life: a masochist in sex will eventually withdraw in all other activities. He will eventually be so moved by the sense of dominance that he will suffer, he will never be fully what he is capable of being.

I first got it on in the army. I was an MP no big deal I mean there was nothing great about it image-wise, but I got it on with other MP's who happened to be as young as me and who happened to be handsome and who weren't neurotic. I mean they were guys who got it on with men and women and even animals I guess small-town farm boys who were filled with a highly charged desire that found its escape through any form of simple sexual contact . . . look at that, there's probably nothing more lonesome than being a drag queen out in the rain hustling the cars along the West Side Highway on Christmas morning . . . see most of the guys I meet out here in the city want to be fucked . . . it's ridiculous they come home with me and flop over on their bellies and want me to ram it up their asses. Now I like to fuck but when I fuck a guy I want to feel that I'm fucking masculinity that the guy beneath me is a guy who has a sense of himself as a man. That's why fucking in a standing position is so great cause one guy isn't on top of the other, there's no sense of dominance or submission other than what's always involved in one body penetrating another but that can be absolved by trading roles so that both men are equal in each other's eyes. I tell ya though even these toughs you meet along the river they put on these hard mannerisms and tell ya they want to fuck you but as soon as you get into bed with them they change their minds they take one look at you and if you happen to have a big cock they want it up their asses . . . I don't mean to say there's something wrong with getting fucked. When I was younger I wanted to get fucked all the time but it was doing something to my head because it was so one-sided there wasn't the necessary opposite force involved. So now that I'm getting older I find I have less sex because I'm choosy. I don't often find guys who will get turned on to the idea of an equal trade-off of force like that which is involved in boxing naked with boots and gloves on and nothing else it's hard to meet a guy who will do it this way. I mean I don't have any kind of uniform to attract the kind of guy I desire. I can't get into wearing any hankies or visored caps or whatever . . . but I feel attracted to you but you'll have to make up your mind if you can get into this scene. I realize it's selfish because it's basically my fantasy but that's all I'm interested in exploring because the form of it as I explained will only make us stronger . . . we'll both be driven to extreme points but it will be equal and simultaneous . . .

Man Lying Back on a Couch in 90-Degree Weather

BROOKLYN

Once I found four grand in Canadian money. I was scuffling around the city one night . . . it was pretty cold out and I started walking up Seventh Avenue trying to find something worth money . . . I wasn't feeling too good. Well up around Carnegie Hall I put my hands deep into my coat and turned around to walk back. I figured, Ah hell no use wasting my time out here. I lived down on the Lower East Side, Avenue C and Tenth Street, so I went all the way downtown, down Fifth Avenue most of the way and then switched over to another avenue where there were a lot of hotels like the Albert and the Edgar. I would case the cars and hotels cause sometimes they'd have something in them. Those hotels back then were pretty fancy . . . not the dumps they are now. So anyway I saw this big station wagon with its windows covered with these whiskey ads: Canadian Club and some other ones. It was parked right in front of the hotel so I crossed over and checked it out. There in the front seat I saw these money bags filled with Canadian cash. There were also a few cases of whiskey in the backseat and at first I thought the money was fake, you know, part of an ad campaign, after all the windows were plastered with these posters. So I grabbed the money there were coins too but they aren't worth anything so I didn't bother and I grabbed two bottles of whiskey to boot. I figured if the money wasn't worth anything at least I could pick up a few bucks for the booze. So Jeanne and Joe and I got in a car, Jeanne was hurting in a bad way, and we went up to Canada but the border guards wouldn't let us in. Jeanne was really young at that time, a beautiful young girl, and the border people took one look at her in the car, she was sitting between Joe and me, they took one look at me and one look at Joe, we looked like pretty rough guys, and that was it, they were afraid that maybe we were taking her out of the country against her will. So we ended up spending a week in a small hotel on the border surrounded by these beautiful pines and small rushing streams. And the people who ran the hotel baked these fresh homemade pies for us . . . it was quite beautiful . . .

Twenty-five-year-old Guy at YMCA Two Weeks after Self-Imposed Hermitude in a Boarded-Up House in New Orleans

SAN FRANCISCO

I worked and saved up enough money to buy a house ... I hate work because I have to please people and I have to worry about them firing me when they find out I'm a homosexual. I can't be bothered with pretending that I'm straight. I mean straight is okay if you're straight but I hate the manic ways men go about proving they're virile whenever a woman walks by and then they expect me to do the same and it becomes complicated so I can't work in one place too long. I hold a job for a few months and then that's it. In New Orleans I managed to work enough to save for a house and then I withdrew into it. The neighbors tried to get rid of me cause for the first couple of months I rented to a few musicians and they were the first blacks to ever come into the area. They were up at all hours beating on their instruments and having loud wine parties. I had the other half of the house and I'd moved into the smallest room cause I wanted to prepare myself for being able to live in the smallest space possible. All I had in there was a mattress on the floor and a rocking chair. I need a rocking chair, it's something that I grew up with in the South. My father and I would sit on the rocker on the front porch and rock for hours and hours watching the changing light and the sun going down and the neighborhood slowly moving indoors. I sat on my rocker in my room most of the time and rolled joints and rocked and rocked. One time I rocked for twenty-eight hours straight just to see how long I could do it. A couple of months later the musicians moved out because nobody would sell them food at the stores around there and they were tired of it. I was kinda glad they moved out because I really wanted to be alone . . .

Most of the people in that neighborhood were into manicuring their lawns and putting up plastic on the outside of their houses but my lawn grew big weeds and after the first year people were complaining and when I'd go into the supermarket they'd try to get me out as fast as they could. I'd hear them talking about me and insulting me but I'd just buy what I had to buy and go home. For a year I saved every piece of garbage left over from the stuff I bought, nothing that would rot but cans plastic wrappings bags. I put them into one room and after a year I couldn't believe it. It was ceiling to floor garbage . . .

I burned all my writings after the first year in that house because I didn't want them to know what I was thinking. If you have no possessions except a couple of clothes and a little food they'll never know what you think. I mean it was like what Dylan says in "It's Alright, Ma (I'm Only Bleeding)": that if they could see what's behind his eyes they'd bring him to the guillotine . . . I used to listen to Dylan a lot . . . I was so happy the first time I heard one of his records. It was as if Dylan was me . . . all that time before I had thought about things that I could never explain to people and when I first listened to a Dylan record it was like he said everything for me, all the fears and stuff about the things I saw in this country . . . I mean about how powerful this government is and how it's programming everybody without them realizing it. But I didn't buy any of Dylan's records after "Lay Lady Lay" came out. Come on! what's this shit? this isn't Dylan. He no longer spoke to me in the lyrics. They weren't important anymore. I think Dylan is controlled now . . . so it's like you can't change anything. They're too powerful. I'm sick of being around people who say they're changing things. They're doing it all wrong. I'm waiting to die and while I'm waiting for that to happen I'm going to sit and watch while they do themselves in. I mean it's going to fall apart after a while because they're pushing in that direction . . . for years I feared death but I realize that this body is just a karmic vehicle for this lifetime and that I was meant to go through all of this . . . I thought about suicide for a while but I don't want to cut a life short of its planned term, the consequences are too dangerous . . . but I am ready for death. Somebody could break open the door to this room right now and rush at me with a knife and slash my stomach open I would just sit here, maybe smile and look at my stomach but I wouldn't try to stop the person because that's the way I was meant to go. My father died a few months ago and he didn't say a word to me for years and years even when I lived in the same house with him. He didn't understand what I was or what I was doing. My mother was glad when he died cause she just wanted the inheritance and to live with her lady friend. I mean she was a lesbian but could never accept it and she lied even to herself all these years, but now that my father's dead she can finally do what she wants. My father was a direct descendant of English royalty . . . the present queen of England's great-grandfather was my father's great-grandfather . . . my father married a woman whose father was black and mother was white and the Royal Family was upset. The marriage took place sometime in the '20s and my father was immediately disowned and monies cut off but he continued to live with my mother and had two children . . . so I'm part Negro . . . I can see it as I get older . . . my features are changing and my skin is getting darker . . . look at my hands my belly they're getting darker. My father died about a month ago and the funeral was ridiculous. My mother hated him but at the wake she put on a big show so that nobody would realize what she really felt. My mother and my brother bought a set of new clothes but not me, I don't get that way about death . . . the show routine . . . I had on a pair of old dungarees and a cotton shirt. My mother waited till all the people arrived then went into hysterics and threw herself onto the open coffin . . . she felt she was supposed to look uncontrollably upset so she started mumbling and making noises and smoothing the hair on his forehead. I walked over and said: Come on, cut it out, and I took her by the arm and threw her into the chair. I was pissed off that she was putting on a show. She stopped her noises immediately and looked at me like she wanted to kill me. Everybody got up and left and my mother went home with my brother. Well, they tried to lock me out of the house. First they wouldn't give me part of the inheritance . . . my mother had papers signed to keep me from touching what I was supposed to get . . . then they locked all the windows and doors and figured that would keep me out. So I smashed the glass and climbed inside to take money out of my mother's purse and eat everything in the refrigerator even when I wasn't hungry as often as I wanted. One day when I came into the kitchen my mother said she was going to call the police if I didn't leave. I told her I wasn't going to do anything but eat and take some money and then I'd leave but she started screaming and trying to hit me and I grabbed her by the throat then my brother came in and grabbed me and put my head into the wall. They called the police and told me to leave. I said: That's okay. I want the police to come. Call them. I continued eating my sandwich while the two of them screamed at me and finally the police arrived and ended up arresting me for disturbing the peace. Can you believe that? Here I was eating a sandwich perfectly calm and those two were screaming and I was arrested for disturbing the peace. Well that's when I spent time in jail three days and my mother had them transfer me to the mental hospital and they ran me through some tests. They hooked me up to electric shock machines that had red brain waves, dozens of these little electrodes attached to my scalp . . . I still have this feeling that they left some of those wires inside my head so they can pick up on what I'm thinking about . . . I know that sounds crazy but that's what I feel at times. When I did something wrong there they would beat me up or make me feel terrible . . . I'd do what I wanted over and over until they left me alone they couldn't get at what I was thinking and they knew I would never stop doing what I wanted. They had my mother come in and talk to them and ended up talking to her more than they talked to me. They told me afterwards that she was the one who really needed to be there not me, so they re-leased me a few hours later. I thought about it for a while and decided that the only reason I was living there was to be near my father and now that he was dead and my mother and brother didn't want me around I might as well sell the house and go to California . . . this is where I want to be anyway . . .

Young Boy in
Seafood Restaurant

NEW YORK CITY

My friend and I hang out down here in the Square all the time . . . it's better than goin to Yankee Stadium. I don't give a fuck about baseball anyway . . . we know a lot of people on this street . . . we can get into almost any movie on the block for free and some of the whores buy us cigarettes and give us money for the game room cause we let them know when the cops are coming. Sometimes there's nothin to do if we have no money so we let some of these guys around here buy us meals. They think we're gonna go to some hotel with them but we split after we eat. We don't like those fuckin guys who wanna take pictures of us. See this. It's a pen right? Well look, it folds down into a knife. If any of those guys bother us about strippin for pictures we just pull this out and tell them to fuck off. They don't bother us that much anymore . . . hey ya see that guy over there? He's into bein treated like a slave. He came up to me and my friend yesterday and took us in here for sodas. We sat in that back booth. He was tellin us he wanted to pay us to come up to his place in Brooklyn and he'd be our slave for the day

. . . he told us he liked to be ordered around, not sex or nothin but like makin us drinks or food. He said he likes bein told what to do . . . another friend of mine knows him. He said that that guy had him and some of his friends in the back of an empty laundry truck one summer. They ordered him to take off his clothes and when he did they tied him up. He thought they were gonna let him go after they were finished but they left him in the truck and took off. So yesterday after we hung out with him for a while my friend stood up and shouted: Buy us hamburgers! and he got really pissed. He said: No no don't do that here . . . I never act like a slave in the street. Ya gotta come home with me, that's the only place I do it. So we split and went over to the Horn & Hardart instead. There's these deaf-mutes there and they pay you twenty dollars to go to a hotel and let them lay on top of you. They don't even get a fuckin hard-on they just make believe that they're fuckin and after a couple of minutes they give you the money. So we did that . . . we get around okay . . . there's always some place to get money . . . once ya hang around down here ya find out from a lot of the other kids but ya gotta watch out cause they got a lot of cops around now . . . some TV station did a film on the Square and now the cops go around in a van and arrest ya if they think you're hustlin . . .

Elderly Transvestite on
Second Avenue (Evening)

NEW YORK CITY

Those muthafuckers got outta jail last night but they'll never come near me again ... they got three years probation apiece ... yeah last week honey this muthafucka comes up and hits me, I got marks all over my arm here, and his girlfriend Camille that white bitch comes and grabs my purse with thirty-five dollars in it. Honey let me tell ya I went straight down to the police station. I don't fool around. I had five detectives plainclothes ones waiting in a car for em ... that guy the Puerto Rican one, he's sittin there against the fence of the church and they jammed outta the car. His girl wasn't around. I said Oh, she'll be right back I know she just got in a car to give some guy a blow job and make ten bucks. The two of them they're dope addicts honey, let me tell you, they handcuffed him to the fence and got back in the car and waited and sure enough in five or ten minutes this blue car comes pullin up and she steps out and she didn't see her boyfriend was handcuffed and the detectives walk right up to her and say You're under arrest and she has the nerve to say What for? She points to the driver of the car and says he's a friend of mine, just drove me here, so they took the two of em down to the station. They spent a week in jail and just got out last night. They come walkin up while I was sittin here and you know what she says to me? She says Well thanks a lot because of you I got three years probation. I said Look, don't you fuck with me cause I'll walk over to that phone and dial the precinct and they'll have your ass in jail in a minute. They won't mess with me. The only thing they can do is kill me, cause if they don't kill me no matter what they do I'll go down to that precinct and bring charges if I want to. They're sitting a few blocks down by the church now. I just seen em there a little while ago . . . I don't mess around . . . let me tell ya honey. I got the cops all the cops in this city in my corner. They know me. They see me comin and they say Don't you come back in here bitch. After they arrested Camille and Juan I went down to court and the judge he said to me Try and stay clear of that area of town, you know over by the church. They all know me down-town baby, down at that courthouse. I spend a lotta time in court . . . I know the law honey . . . I know the law real well . . . I'm a lawyer ya know. Why I'm helpin out a lot of the people down along here. I'm helping some person over here prepare a case. I interviewed them and I got the papers typed up in my purse . . . see my new purse? some woman gave it to me and lookit this honey . . . someone came up and gave me this tonight. It's a pants suit . . . lookit this nice jacket . . . it'll be good for the wintertime . . . they all know me around here, honey . . . they all treat me real good . . .

Canada-bound Trucker
on Interstate 90

NEW YORK

I was a coast-to-coast trucker for twenty-five years . . . lemme tell ya it's hard work . . . I mean I know they put out these books makin truckin life look glamorous but it ruins ya . . . if I had the choice to do it all over again I wouldn't choose it but what can I do now . . . I can't quit it . . . not with that pension I'm buildin up . . . I'm forty-five and I gotta do this north-south drivin for another thirteen years before I can retire . . .

I seen a lot of strange things drivin coast to coast. This one time I stopped off at a truckers' rest stop, this big restaurant refuelin place I would drop by whenever I was goin through Arizona. I stopped off and there were these two kids who couldn't have been more than eighteen or twenty years old. The railroad bulls had caught them ridin boxcars and beat the hell out of them . . . this one kid had a big white bloody patch over the side of his head. They beat them up with clubs and threw them in jail for a week . . . so this one kid came up to me and started beggin me: Listen, man, the cops beat us up and run us off the freights and we tried hitchin and got thrown in jail. We ain't got no money and we've been in this stop for three days. We can't go out to the highway to hitch or we'll land in jail again. Ya gotta help us out cause I swear if I don't get a ride soon I'm gonna go out and steal a car. I can't take it no more. I haven't eaten in three days and I got no family to call for help. I felt awful but I couldn't take them. My partner was with me and we had no room . . .

There ain't hoboes like there used to be . . . I remember hoboes . . . real ones . . . used to be out on the roads all the time . . . we'd give them lifts in the trucks when we were travelin alone. Boy I'll tell ya these guys had the gift of bull. They'd tell ya stories from here till tomorrow. I'd pick up guys who were dentists scientists teachers doctors, a lot of them had good educations and high-payin jobs at some time or other but then somethin happened and they started on the bottle. I picked up this one hobo once who told me that he had been with NASA at one point. He was with them when they were buildin the first rockets to put up into space and he was gettin quite a bundle of money and had a wife and two kids and then outta nowhere he finds out his wife was havin an affair with some guy. Turned out the guy was his boss, the fella he worked for at NASA. He said he and his boss were real good friends too and this was goin on be-hind his back so he started hittin the bottle and quit his job and left for the road. He told me he was goin on back to Florida soon, that's where his wife and two kids lived, but he wasn't gonna look them up cause he didn't want his sons to see what kind of guy he ended up as . . . no aims left in the world and no desire to do anything with his life just drinkin himself away . . .

Ya see somethin happens in their lives and they end up not wantin to do anything but move on get away from everything and everybody. They don't even wanna work again for nobody . . . they don't wanna be around anybody for too long . . . just movin on when things get crowded . . . movin from town to town and drinkin their wine . . . that's all . . . that way they don't have to face any of it . . . they don't recognize any of their past in anything . . . they consider life one big zero and they themselves show what they think by becoming the same thing . . . no aim and no point . . .

Man in Sheridan Square Park
Drinking 1:00 A.M.

NEW YORK CITY

I can dance ... I can dance ... lemme tell ya I can dance ... I ain't bullshittin ya ... see that corner over there across the street. Well you just keep your eyes on that corner cause in another two or three weeks I'm gonna be dancin there ... first I gotta get me a pair of leather shoes though ... see these shoes here they ain't shit ... they made of rubber on the soles ... I need a pair of real leather shoes for dancin ... I just got back from Florida ... been down there for three years ... just got back a couple of weeks ago ... lemme tell ya this straight slim ... I hope ya don't mind me callin ya slim ... see I was a dancer for years ... I do real dancin not any of that where you shake your ass and do that boogaloo bullshit but real dancin soft-shoe tap ... I can do some mean steps ... I'd do some for ya if I had a pair of leather shoes ... I could show you some fancy steppin and slidin. Ya know how ya slide on roller skates? Well I could show you a slide on my heel where I do a fancy step like this and then I could slide from here to that manhole cover just on my heel alone ... I bet you never seen dancin like that. I learned to tap in the Savoy Ballroom up in Harlem in 1956 . . . bet you was just a kid then . . . well I loved watchin them movies with Fred Astaire. Fred was my idol but see I feel bad cause he had the chance I'll never have and I know I coulda outstepped him . . . I could do a step that would upset Texas . . . now I'm serious. I could do a step that would have Texas come all the way up here to New York and arrest me it would be so good . . . see all I'm trying to do with this cola cup here is get a little money up to buy me a pair of real leather shoes . . . then I'd be on that corner I'd chalk up a square the size of this sidewalk and I'd have me a fine time steppin . . . I'd have all these people's attention right away . . . see that? lemme tell ya I seen all sorts of stuff standing on this corner. I just came down from Grant's Tomb and the Jazzmobile this after-noon . . . I be standing here on the corner and these two men come by and start kissin each other right here on the street . . . two men . . . and I be lookin around and here they are tonguing each other. Now I'm lost . . . I don't understand that shit but that's their game I won't be callin them up on their game. Hell I'd be in a whole lot of trouble I'd have some argument on my hands if I woulda said somethin so I just kept lookin around don't pay attention to none of it . . . but it ain't my scene lemme tell ya slim . . . if I had me a pair of leather shoes I'd cut that shit out right away . . . they'd be forgettin about kissin and watchin me . . . lemme tell ya I know how to dance . . . I was a star once . . . hear this slim, for a while all you see is stars and then ya don't see nothin . . . that's how it goes . . .

Boy in Horn & Hardart's
on Forty-second Street

NEW YORK CITY

There's this guy who hangs out down here, usually hangs out with a bunch of gangsters. One of the guys he hung out with had his own private phone at a window table in the Child's Coffee Shop across the street. About a week and a half ago I was cutting school and I ran into him in Nathan's. He bought me a cup of coffee and we talked for a while and then he invited me up to his place . . . he lived up in the Eighties somewhere between Amsterdam and Columbus Avenue so we went up there and got into bed, this was about five o'clock, we were having sex when there was this pounding on the door. We stopped and kept real quiet for a few seconds then he says: Who is it? and there was some more pounding and someone yelled: Open up it's the police! I said: Oh shit what'll we do? The two of us jumped up and started pullin on our clothes and I kept thinking: Oh god what'll my parents say when the police call them up and I pulled on my pants and didn't bother with my underwear and he was whispering something about being on parole for something. The police started ramming the door like they were gonna break it down so I grabbed my sneakers and my socks and put my shirt on and ran to the back window . . . we were on the second floor and his windows opened onto a big court-yard it ran the whole length of the block and there was no way out except through cellar doors . . . there were a whole bunch of fences and private patios. I threw open the win-dow and tossed my shoes and socks and underwear down onto the concrete and he helped me out and held my arms and lowered me as far as he could reach and then I dropped the rest of the way. I thought I was gonna crack an ankle but I didn't. I picked up my stuff and jumped over the first fence and then a whole bunch more . . . I kept trying basement doorways but they were all locked and I was afraid if I pounded on them someone would call the police so I ran almost the whole block and finally I went down this alley-way that came to a brick wall and there were some boards laying on the ground. I propped them against the wall and hid behind them. I left a little crack between them so I could see if the police came down the alley looking for me. After about twenty minutes I remembered my subway pass in my wallet so I got up and hid it under some other boards further away in the alley, then I crawled behind the boards again and sat there not moving until it got dark. I kept thinking the police would come any minute. When it got late I crawled out and started walking back through the courtyard trying doors on the opposite side. I finally found one building that had been burned out and I could walk through it to the front but there were iron bars over the window and an iron door that had a chain wrapped around the bars with a padlock on it . . . I thought I was gonna go nuts . . . I could see people pass by on the street and I could hear the traffic but I couldn't get out. I went back into the courtyard and turned to the side of the building to try other doors when I saw a light on in a basement apartment. I peeked inside and there was a guy in there sitting in a chair and he was naked and talking on the phone. He was really handsome and I started getting excited. I wanted to knock on the window but I didn't know if he would call the police thinking I was a burglar so after a while I went back into the burned-out building and checked all the window bars to see if there wasn't some way to kick them out. Then suddenly I saw that the padlock on the chain wasn't snapped shut so I quick undid it and opened the iron door and stepped up onto the sidewalk. I walked real slow to the corner and as soon as I turned it I started running . . . I ran from the Eighties all the way down to the Village where I lived . . .

A Kid on the Piers
near the West Side Highway

NEW YORK CITY

He's got me down on my knees and I can't focus on anything I have no time to understand the position of my body or the direction of my face I see a pair of legs in rough corduroy and the color of the pants is brown and surrounded by dark shadows and there's a sense of other people here and yet I can't hear them breathe or their feet move or anything and his hand suddenly comes up against the back of my head and he's got his fingers locked in my hair and he's shoving my face forward and twisting my head almost gentle but very violent behind the gentleness and I only got half a breath in my lungs the smell of piss on the floorboards and this heavy bulge in his pants getting harder and harder as my face is forced against the front of his pants the zipper tearing my lips I feel them getting fat and bruised and all the while he's stroking my face and tightening his fingers around the locks of my hair and I can't focus my eyes my head being pushed and pulled and twisted and caressed and it's as if I got no hands I know I got hands I had hands a half hour ago I remember lighting a cigarette with them and I remember how warm the flame of the match was when I lifted it towards his face and my knees are hurting real bad from the stone floor hurting because they banged on the floor when he dragged me down the cellar stairs I remember a door in the darkness and the breath of his dog as it licked at my hands when I reached out to stop my headlong descent its tongue licking at my fingers and my face slams down and there's this electric blam inside my head and it's like my eyes suddenly opened on one huge bright sun and then went black with the switch thrown down and I'm shocked and there's pressure on my face on my forehead and something cold and wet and his arms come swinging down he's lifting me up saying looking for me? and he buries his face and I feel his saliva running down into the curve of my neck and my arms are hanging loose and my head is way back and I can see a ceiling and a dim bulb tossing back and forth and suddenly I'm on my knees again and my face is getting mashed into his belly and sliding down across rough cloth and the metal zipper and there's this sweet musty smell and I can't breathe and my head is pulled back and his dick is slapping across my eyes and being rubbed over my cheeks and bloody lips and suddenly it's inside my mouth and his hands are twisted up in my hair cradling the back of my skull shoving me forward and I feel his dick hit me in the back of the throat and I start feeling pain for the first time like the open pants are in focus and he's pulled his dick out of my mouth and I'm choking and he's running one big hand over my face putting his fingers in my ears in my mouth dragging down my lower jaw and forcing his dick in between the fingers and the saliva and blood and shoving in and out and pulling on my hair and everything goes out of focus my eyes moving around blindly the smell of basement water and raw sewage and mustiness and he's slapping my face like he wants to wake me up and I realize I'm crying and he tells me that he loves me and he lifts me up and pulls me towards him in a big hug and he puts his lips over mine and sticks his tongue in my mouth and buries his rough face down into my collar and licks and drags his tongue over my neck and shoulders and his hands are up inside my shirt and he's rubbing them back and forth across my chest and belly and taking quick handfuls of flesh and twisting and pulling and then his hands are in the back of my pants to the sides and he suddenly rips apart my pants and punches me in the side of the head at the same time pulling my hair and pulling me back down on the floor and I'm on my belly I feel cold stone scraping my skin and he kneels down onto the center of my back and it hurts and I try to scream but he's shoving my underwear into my mouth and I'm hit with such a feeling of claustrophobia and fear that it's hours before I realize that my hands and legs are tied together and that I'm lying on my side and the rag in my mouth is soaking wet and making small bubbling sounds each time I breathe . . .

Hobo in Train Yard

PASCO, WASHINGTON

tell ya ... if ya got a good story and an unknown face you can pick up ten or twenty dollars' worth of food stamps from this welfare office about a mile from here in town. One time I found this old crutch somebody lost so I limped into this office where this woman was workin and I sat down and told her how my car broke down about ten miles down the road ... I said me and my wife and my three kids had been drivin for days and we ran outta money ... I told her that my wife was real sick and needed to go to a doctor and my kids ain't had nothin to eat for the last couple of days ... I tell ya I almost had that woman cryin ... she was about to reach into her own purse and give me money when this guy comes in who works there and he starts questionin me and after a while they caught on that I was tellin them a story and they told me: Man, you get your crutch and you use it to get out of town cause if we see you around here again we're gonna have you arrested. I was embarrassed and I got the hell outta there as fast as I could. Yesterday I met two young hitchhikers just like yourselves ... they took me out and bought me a nice breakfast and a couple jugs of wine. They were real nice but that wine made me sleepy. This mornin some guy comes into the car bangin on the wall and says: Okay I need me four guys to unload a truck . . . take ya about two hours and I'll pay ten dollars. I rolled over and went back to sleep . . . unloadin a truck in that condition? Well, excuse me . . . I gotta go see if my buddy got paid . . . maybe we'll go into town and bring back a nice bottle of wine . . .

Man in Brew & Burger
on Forty-second Street
and Eighth Avenue

NEW YORK CITY

guess things are going okay . . . a little slow since the convention in Portland. My son is out of the army and finally off drugs . . . he's not so much a problem anymore . . . my wife still gets angry as hell but I don't know what to say to him. I mean he's working fairly regularly, drives a cab, starts around midnight and works till six o'clock in the morning . . . we hardly have words these days because when he gets home around seven he goes right upstairs and hits the sack. Some nights he'll get into an all-night card game with the fellas down at the taxi stand . . . I can't get angry with him . . . I mean, I don't know what he's been going through . . . he used to be a beautiful kid, long hair and built like an athlete. Now he's gained weight he's up to 250 pounds and lays around most of the time drinking beer but he does work. He rides in the car I bought him two years ago . . . god you should see that car now, what a mess, the two sides dented in like a nutcracker squeezed them, the back fenders hanging off and some days the backseat is piled up to the rear ledge with beer cans. My wife gets really upset because she's home all day.

My daughter, she's a real doll, she's a sophomore in college now, she's engaged to this terrific young fella who's with RCA . . . the two of them flew off for a week to the Keys together . . .

Work has been slow for me since the beginning of the year. I feel bad because I'm not pulling my share of the load . . . it's just that there's so much mental activity holding me back . . . I try to stay away from the city . . . I've been pretty successful with doing so . . . I mean I walk down Forty-second Street and I'm sad to say it's changed so much since ten years ago. I can remember that in the summer of '69 you could walk down the block and there were all these beautiful kids hanging out . . . now they're all addicts and in gangs looking to rob you . . . but occasionally I still go to the bars in the upper Forties . . . they have some great music and the dancing kids are really wild, good-looking kids and they move in a great way. But I don't go for the sex in those places . . . it's like two minutes in some smelly dark cabinet and there goes thirty bucks. Where I live I have some wild times . . . there's young boys in their late teens, sixteen or seventeen, hitchhiking all over the place and a lot of them are into sex . . . it's really something I mean I have to keep telling myself that I'm a man with responsibilities . . . I have an outstanding job and a wonderful family . . . I really can't afford to get arrested. I'd lose it all yet I can't help it . . . I mean it's so simple to go for a drive . . . after I pick one of these kids up I work in four sex words into the conversation. There's this one kid who goes to high school just a mile from where I work. I picked him up hitchhiking one time and three minutes later we were in the parking lot of my job in the backseat making love to each other. I've seen him a couple of times a week for a while but I guess he's decided to end it . . . he hasn't shown up in three weeks . . . I drive over to the school every now and then and wait for a half hour or so but I guess he's not going to show up . . .

Guy on Fourteenth Street 3:00 A.M.

NEW YORK CITY

got busted once while I was in my apartment doin acid. I lived in this building that had an intercom but if somebody buzzed I'd just ring em in without askin who they were so the buzzer rang and I pressed the button and two cops in plain clothes came in. They flashed their narc badges and one of them said: We busted Daniel tonight and found your name in his telephone book. Now I really had balls that night . . . I said: Look man if you ain't got a search warrant get the fuck outta here and they were pissed but left. About four days later the doorbell rang and this girl I knew was out there and asked to borrow somethin of mine so I told her come on in. She sat down on the couch and I got the thing for her and she continued sittin there all greased up with a towel around her . . . she was actin kinda dizzy so I finally said: Look I got someone in the other room and she said sorry and left. I saw a pack of cigarettes where she'd been sittin on the couch and I said to the kid: She'll be back she forgot her cigarettes and sure enough the doorbell rang and I took the cigarettes to the door and didn't even look out I just stuck my hand through the door and bam there was a handcuff on it . . . it was the fuckin cops so I said real loud: *Oh, It's the cops* figuring the kid would hear me and flush his stuff down the toilet but he was young and so instead of getting rid of what he was holding he was too busy trying to wash the Vaseline off his ass. The cops threatened to charge me with impairing the morals of a minor and I said: What are ya talkin about? We ain't done a thing and the cops say: Yeah? then why's your dick all greasy? I said: Hey man, my cock's all chapped from the cold weather so I cover it with Vaseline, works great ya oughta try it sometime . . . and man did they kick the shit outta me . . . broke my fuckin nose and busted two ribs . . .

Man Drinking Coffee
in Thirty-third Street Pizzeria

NEW YORK CITY

have had no desire for sex for the last ten years ...
up till ten years ago I'd want to get into bed a lot ... when
I'd see some young cat with a good body I always wanted
to have sex with him ... or with some girl with a beautiful
figure I wanted to put my hands around her but then suddenly I decided I was tired of waking up and feeling that sex
is a head thing ... I mean you use a lot of thoughts in sex
like: What makes this person excited? What turns that person on? It made me very tired and so it just dropped from my
life ... There's this one cat who lives in the building of a
woman I know ... now I never for the world thought that
this guy would be involved with any kind of homosexuality.
He was a fine-looking cat, a real nice-looking guy. One day
he knocked on the door and asked if I would mind him coming in for a chat. I said: Oh no not at all man. I opened the
door for him made us a couple of drinks with vodka and
grapefruit juice and we talked on and on and suddenly he
leans over and puts his hand on my leg and says: Man I want
to go to bed with you. I was shocked and after a moment or

two I said: I'm *really* sorry man but I *can't*. If I got into bed
with you I'd just get you all excited and get myself half excited and it wouldn't work. After a few minutes he got up
and left . . . I felt terrible . . . I sat down and wrote him a long
letter trying to explain all the things that were going through
my head and sent it to him . . . not long afterwards he sent
me a very beautiful letter thanking me for mine . . .

Man in Coffee Shop
Midnight East Village

NEW YORK CITY

Hey, did I ever tell you about the time I got beat up when I was twelve or thirteen years old. It was in Cortland Park. I had gone there fishing with three other friends of mine and these older guys came along, like five or six guys, most of them about fifteen or sixteen and one guy older maybe around eighteen. They took turns beating us up, taking us into the bushes and punching us in the face and all over. One of my friends started crying and then another started crying but I was too furious to cry and then the third guy started crying and I was getting more and more punches in the face and finally I realized that if I could work it up to cry they would probably stop so I forced myself to cry a little bit, then we got split up, me and one friend were taken by the two oldest guys into some other part of the woods. The other guys disappeared and at some point the oldest guy—boy was he good-looking, I didn't think of it then but now years later looking back on it I realize he was a handsome boy with a good body and bluish eyes—well he had us take off our clothes saying somethin about keeping us from running away and then he had us unbutton his pants and take out his cock and then he said: Alright, which one of you has the biggest ass and he looked at both our asses. I remember squeezing real tight so my asshole would be smaller and he decided the other guy's ass was bigger so he fucked the other guy for a while and then tried to fuck me. I remember he couldn't get it in me cause I kept squeezing and so he fucked me between the legs and then he came. I remember it was revolting, his come smeared between my legs. Afterwards he let us go and we had to search around for soda bottles to cash in and get money to take the train home. My face was swollen. I had two black eyes and I was all bruised and scratched. I didn't tell my mother that this guy tried to fuck me but she took me down to the police station and made me report it to the police anyway . . .

Man in Casual Labor Office
6:30 A.M.
SAN FRANCISCO

'm tired of being a tramp . . . my father was a tramp and he's dead . . . I'm a tramp and I don't want to be one . . . I stopped drinking . . . I wear only old-man clothes . . . I wash up every day . . . I work . . . and I'm still a tramp . . . does anybody want to tell me the secret? How do I de-tramp myself? I read Machiavelli and he done me no good . . .

Now my wife, she tried to do me good . . . she thought she could put me away in some asylum . . . you know, what's the name of that place up north of here? . . . well anyway she said to the neighbors: You think I can't put him away? You just wait and see. So she cooked me a fine meal . . . ummm, it was good and when I came home she said: Baby, you just sit down and lemme take care of you. So I sat down and ate and after dinner she drew me a bath with all that bubble stuff in it and then she said: Now you wash up and I'll wait for you in the bedroom. So I took the bath and when I finished I walked into the bedroom and she was lying there with her silks on and her legs spread apart . . . mmm, she took care of me real good . . . then when we finished she said: Baby, why don't we go for a ride okay? I said: Why? and she said: Cause I want you to meet somebody in that hospital on top of the hill. So I said: Okay let's go and we drove up to the hospital parked in the lot and went inside. We were walking down the hall and I see this group of attendants walking towards us . . . I knew what the bitch had in mind so I quick reached down and took hold of her skirt and pulled it up over her head and started shouting: *"Hey you. Over there. Quick grab this woman she's crazy and I've been trying to commit her."* So she was screaming and they took her and locked her up . . . she's been there twenty years now . . . I'm the one who's crazy and they got her in there and they won't let her go till I sign her out . . .

Man on Interstate
Heading Towards NYC

We have plenty of time so I'll start from the beginning . . . see I was managing about thirty-eight stores at the World's Fair and making some decent money. It meant working for the mob . . . and around that time I met this beautiful guy, a burly football jock with translucent skin all cock and no brains but he was sweet. He was one of those guys who didn't think he was—I hate to use the word *gay* can't stand it but for the moment let's say it: gay—I made it with him but he still considered himself straight . . . around that time while I was managing these stores someone came up to me and said: Hey I figured out this system for roulette that's unbeatable and he gave me the system and there was this guy working for me in one of the stores, sleazy slick pool shark kind of guy and mean too but smart so I took this system to him and said: Hey Sal check this out and let me know what you think, will it work? Sal checked it out and said: Look, it's an old system it'll work for you for a while but eventually you'll get cleaned out. It just doesn't work for long. So me and Sal and the jock got a whole lot of money together, we stole a lot of it, and took off to Puerto Rico. We moved into a hotel but Sal didn't want any part of our scene he wanted to be alone so me and the jock moved into another hotel not far from his near the casino districts. For the first few weeks we'd each take some of the money and go out to the different casinos and work them using this system. It was great, we were making a thousand a night, we got pretty well known at the casinos. We'd be there every night and it got so that the croupiers hated us couldn't stand the sight of us but we were having a ball making lots of money spending lots of money. The jock was delirious we were all excited and having fun but after about six weeks I started getting a little crazy, bored with the whole scene and then one night I was working the tables and this entertainer from one of the nearby hotels showed up and played. He was playing against the house and I was playing with the house. Do you know what that means? So he was taking even numbers and I was taking odds with the house and well, do you know what the record is for throwing straight passes, for throwing the dice like evens so many times in a row? Well the record was something like thirty straight passes and this guy threw twenty-seven straight passes in a row and I was putting a lot of money down and by the end of the evening we were cleaned out, had absolutely no money and to tell you the truth I wasn't upset at all, Sal was pissed off, the jock was upset but I felt relieved, like it was the answer to everything and I didn't have to deal with it anymore.

So we split up ... Sal disappeared got himself into some trouble and ended up in La Princhessa, that was the name for the worst prison on the island. This prison was situated on the bottom of a cliff and guys used to go over to the top and look over and the inmates would jerk themselves off through the bars of the window screaming and yelling all sorts of stuff. Anyway Sal ended up in La Princhessa, but we didn't find out about it till later . . . we didn't know where he was he just disappeared and me and the jock ran into some American woman who had a condominium on the beach and a couple of kids and her husband had just left her. They were in the midst of a messy divorce and she had something like sixty bucks left to her name and her rent was due and right around then I met this French woman who was trying to get off the island before she got deported. She was having some trouble over something but was pretty much broke and she had the lease to this bar that was closed down, a street-corner bar and I asked her how much she needed and she said about fifty bucks and I said: How about handing over the lease to the bar and I'll give you the fifty bucks and she said: Sure okay so I went back to the American woman and got fifty bucks from her and traded it for the lease to the bar and with the other ten bucks we got these cards printed up saying good for one free drink at The Bar on the corner of Valencia and such 'n' such and we went into the bar and covered the front of the door on the outside with a thick piece of black velvet and put a door knocker in the center of it, covered the windows, bought some ice and cans of Coca-Cola and a few bottles of cheap rum something like fifty cents for a fifth and after that we put a spotlight over the front door aiming it at the knocker and then we went down to the beach passing out the cards to everyone we saw: drag queens people from the circus and tattooed guys and the jock got into what I was doing and he handed out some too and then we opened the bar and the place was filled, packed with every freak on the island. We had gone downtown to a jukebox joint and gotten one so the place was hopping every night and some of the characters from the sideshow of the circus made it their hangout and this one drag queen got a flamenco dress left to her in a will and she showed up and we had her dancing on tables to the songs from the jukebox and one time a giant from the circus showed up. He was taller than any basketball player but not really a giant, and he got a blow job from the flamenco dancer in the middle of the bar one night. Things were going well I never had any trouble or anything until one night when this Puerto Rican guy said: Hey how come you got yourself a bar and I'm Puerto Rican and I ain't got one and I said, Hell I did it with fifty bucks you can raise the money go open your own and one night this guy threw a knife at me and it just missed my head flew right past me and stuck in the wall so I grabbed this lead pipe we kept behind the counter and hopped over the bar yelling: Turn on the work lights and the guy ran through the door into the street screaming: Policia Policia. Other than that I never had any trouble . . . a couple of guys here or there would try to lay some muscle on me but I usually could talk my way out of any situation . . . so around then things were going great, the bar was a success and me and the jock were living with the American woman and he fell in love with her. I remember one night we were lying in bed and he rolled over towards me in his sleep and I went down on him and it just drove him up the wall. He flipped out about it and I said: Who needs this shit and got my stuff together and left Puerto Rico . . .

Woman in Coffee Shop

SAN FRANCISCO

Man I'll tell you . . . they wouldn't take me down under a hundred grams . . . shit my habit was big when I walked in there . . . the first day they tried to take me down ten grams . . . hell they can't get away with that, with that new law that came into effect . . . I threw myself down on the floor and started screaming: Aghhh, uhhnn, I'm sick, I'm sick. Shit man they can't take me down till I'm ready. Ya know today I checked out my file got a look at it and it said I don't give in at all . . . like when I'm in an argument about something even when it becomes ridiculous, you know like when I know I'm wrong, I still give reasons and arguments no matter what I don't admit that I'm wrong. It said a lot of other shit too like about when I went to jail for the first time I walked in there and I was scared cause they got a lotta big women . . . they sit around and as soon as the door opens they say: Aahhhaaa, look at this young turkey look at her, so small and young. And they start laying for ya man just like it is in men's prisons. Five broads holding your arms and legs while one goes down on your box . . . especially if you're small like I am ya know man. Like Louie now he had a lotta problems with that kinda stuff cause he's small, shit he had to bang someone on their head with a board soon as he got in jail cause otherwise they'll getcha . . . hell he even got in trouble for settin fire to someone with hair tonic or aftershave or some shit like that . . . ha ha . . . I shoulda looked around for a two-by-four to carry around everywhere with me . . .

Boy in YMCA

SAN FRANCISCO

arrived here by Greyhound . . . I had one of them Ameri-
pass tickets . . . it was good for two months. I started out
in New York City . . . figured they wouldn't be able to follow me if I rode the bus . . . I didn't stay in one city too long
and I'd decide what direction I was gonna go in only after I
was at the bus station but they would always find out where
I was going and follow me. I'd get on the bus choose a seat
by myself and look out the window. At first the people who
got on looked normal, like I didn't know them and they'd
act like they didn't know me. Then after an hour or so they'd
all be talking in conversations between themselves and would
start to let little words or sentences slip into the conversations . . . things that only I would know about, little refer-
ences to what happened in New York . . . like I knew this
guy . . . we were lovers and after a year of living together he
suddenly didn't want to live with me anymore. I was really
upset and I knew his parents didn't know he was a homosexual so I called his mother up and told her . . . I knew it
was fucked up but I didn't think about it . . . another time I

called the police on a guy I knew ... there was some mur-
derer going around. I told the police that he was the one doing
it ... he was a dealer and when the cops got in his apartment they found the stuff ... I felt guilty about it and tried
suicide. I swallowed this bottle of some kind of pills and just
got really sick ... Then I realized that's what they wanted
me to do so I left New York but they always catch up to me
... I'm really tired of running ... I have no more money and
this is the end of the line for me ... I don't know exactly
what I'm gonna do ... I wish I would die ... that's all I'm
waiting for now ... I can't do it myself but I don't want to go
on existing ... just waiting for it to happen. Everywhere I go
I find people who I think might not be part of the plan ...
then after a while I begin to realize that they're just acting
like strangers ... they're just waiting for me to do it ... like
you ... I don't know why I'm talking to you ... for a few
minutes I thought you were okay ... but as I keep talking I
see little things going on in your expressions so I'm not really
sure ...

... I keep having these strange dreams ... last night I
dreamt that I was a giant ... I was draped over the planet ...
my head rested on North America and my legs rested on South
America ... my arms stretched for miles and miles over the
oceans ... and I could feel millions of fish just below the
surface of the water ... I could feel them nibbling on my
arms ... real gentle ...

Man in Lower East Side
Tenement Room

NEW YORK CITY

One night during the summer I was in the park and all of a sudden it started pissing rain I mean raining hard . . . all the regulars took off and I was left standing there alone. I was still cruising and this kid appeared we were both drenched and he said hello . . . well we talked for a few minutes and then he mentioned money and I said No, I'm not about that and I was leaving the park when he called out something. I turned and he called me back over and asked me if I had enough to get some beer and I said Yeah. He was about twenty, a Puerto Rican kid, absolutely gorgeous, sorta moved like this, with his arms out with this loping gait so we left the park and he starts walking north and I say Where the hell you going and he says he knows of an all-night deli further up around Twenty-first Street . . . so we walk uptown in the rain and we get to the deli. Finally we get this quart of beer and we start walking downtown again and he's going off about this and that and somewhere along the way he stops to talk to this hooker and share the quart of beer with her . . . we finally get here I bring him back

to my place . . . that was when I didn't have any electricity I
had told him this but I guess he didn't believe me so when
we get back here he's sort of surprised. I had all these candles
lit in the room and it was pretty dark . . . he liked that chair
over there and he sat in it while we talked . . . then he looks
out the window at the mission house and says Man, it's not
very nice to look out there or something like that and Man,
you have to fix this place up . . . and at some point I mention
that I do some acting and he starts telling me about his family about his mother and his grandmother and there was this
knife of mine on the table and he picks it up as he's talking
and then he starts imitating them, acting out the role of his
grandmother as he's talking about her, I mean it was scary,
this whole sort of ritualistic thing passing the knife back and
forth as he's acting out parts of this movie talking in different
voices and flashing his eyes . . . it was pure voodoo . . .

I brought him back here a couple of times and mentioned
him to other people I know . . . then one time I was in the
park and he showed up and I didn't want anything to do with
him so I left and he followed me out and started demanding
money. I just happened to have about forty bucks on me so
I said Sure okay I can give you a few bucks and I gave him
some and he kept following me and then he wanted a beer
so I stopped in a deli and bought him a bottle of beer and
wanted to get rid of him so I walked on ahead of him and
instead of coming around Second Avenue it's too dangerous
that way at night I walked up Fourth Street to the Bowery
and then cut down to Third Street. I didn't see him anywhere
so I figured he was gone well I get near my building and I
spot him sitting out in front in a car drinking the beer. I
thought Uh oh. So I go into my building and he caught me
between the two doors and said Let's go up to your place
and I said No, look I'm tired I'm going to go to sleep he said
Look do I have to rough you up or are you going to let me

come upstairs? so once he got inside he started demanding money. I got up from the couch and went into the kitchen and tried to get rid of the money in my pocket. I fumbled doing it. He threatened me and then he said he was gonna start picking up my cats and throwing them out the window so I gave him the money . . . I had some pot here and he took that and sat down and started rolling joints . . . I told him I was tired and wanted to go to sleep, I asked him to leave but he wouldn't . . . then he got up and went into the bathroom he did this several times during the time he was here and at one point I told him I was really tired and going to sleep and got into bed and lay down and closed my eyes I didn't sleep I couldn't do that but I lay down and he came back into the room and started throwing money on the table and the floor and then finally he left. As he was leaving he said I'll be back and I said No you won't. You can't come back here . . .

I would get phone calls from him every once in a while up until just a month ago he would call me collect from St. Mark's. I'd get this operator saying Will you accept a collect call from Jose or Stanley? his name was Ricardo but he would call up using these assumed names. One time he called up having actually deposited a dime in the phone and I said Hello Ricardo and he said I wanna come over and I said No you can't and he said Look man you owe me ten bucks . . .

Girl Sitting on Pavement
in Front of Coffee Shop

ALBUQUERQUE

I live in a hotel a few miles from here ... I come down just about every day since I quit my job ... I was working as a waitress in a restaurant downtown ... worked at it for two years ... I don't know how I did it for so long ... it's like the time just went by behind my back. Before I became a waitress I hitched all over the U.S. . . . I'm originally from San Antonio ... my family still lives there and I hate the place ... the people there are almost dead ... all into their little trips with the way they think lives should run ... the way their folks taught them ... my father had a lot of money and my two sisters got married real young ... I didn't want nothing to do with the whole apron thing ... I just wanted to run around ... I mean there's just so much going on in the States alone that it makes me dizzy to think of what I'm missing sitting here. My father said he'd cut me out of the will if I didn't go to school so I split ... it's kinda romantic I mean I've been hitching for the past five years ... lived just about everywhere and mostly followed the migrant people picking produce and stuff. What got to me was that it was only romantic because I had the choice ... I mean there was security behind me if I chose to go back ... but no, I was tough and could make it on my own. So I worked this waitress job because I was tired and I thought maybe I could settle down and do some thinking instead of all that continuous experiencing but man after two years of serving all those people ... let me tell you there's two things in life people get really bitchy about: one's money and the other's their food ... I'd hassle with these people over food and then sit down and like the counter is over here and the kitchen is over there and the windows are here and the door is there ... that's the only part of the job I really liked ... walking out that fucking door. I mean everything's outside and I was thinkin how much it picked me up to walk through the door so I said: That's it I quit I have money saved up not a whole lot but enough to make some plans to go somewhere else. Right now I'm just taking it easy and thinking. I come down here because there's a lot going on on this street ... all these people rushing around helps me to make sense, to see how to live. This afternoon I was sitting out here watching those prostitutes across the street and one of them stepped out of the doorway and took this little guy with a guitar by the hand, he had just jumped off some dump truck from Arizona, she took him by the hand really gentle like he was a kid going to school for the first time and they walked down the street to the hotel together, him carrying this guitar without a case, like he played that guitar all around the country just to end up in some squeaky bed in a ratty hotel where somebody's gonna hold him for a while, even for ten minutes ya know ... and like I felt kind of sad because that's really it ... it's never any more than that scene ... and when it becomes more ... then the whole idea of measure in your life is forgotten ... you never make sense of nothing ...

Guy Waiting for a Bus

NEW JERSEY

This friend of mine went on a trip to Portugal last summer ... he was there for a few weeks ... one day he was walking on this beach along a stone wall where all these natives were walking around carrying large machetes, they use them to cut down bananas, well this one guy came up to my friend and pulled his machete on him and robbed him. My friend gave him forty dollars which was all he had on him. The guy dragged him over the stone wall where they couldn't be seen then he pointed the machete at my friend's crotch and went into this harangue about the rich tourists who fuck over the country ... the guy demanded more money and my friend told him, I don't have any more if I had ten thousand dollars I'd give it to you ... the guy went back into his harangue and kept the machete on him and started pulling off his pants ... he told my friend he wanted a blow job ... my friend started crying and begging him to let him go but the guy continued taking off his pants ... just then my friend remembered something a friend of his had told him ... so he gets down on his knees and clasps his hands

together and starts praying out loud to all the saints and religious figures he could think of: Oh please St. Francis Mother
Mary of God St. Peter ... the guy freaked out ... his eyes
got wide and he stumbled into his pants and jumped over
the stone wall got into a taxicab and split ...

Hobo on Flatcar
Eastbound for St. Paul

MINNEAPOLIS

I came east from Spokane Washington last night . . . been riding all night headin to St. Paul to a mission so I can get a meal and some sleep . . . ya gotta watch these overpasses at night . . . *it's dangerous* . . . them kids who live up around here'll attack ya or stone ya to death . . . there's no lights in these cars and these kids think there's nothin funnier than to jump some guy and beat him up or hit him in the head with rocks . . . hey ya see that guy come outta that tunnel? ya know where he just came from? Well a lot of them homosexuals come down to this area to have what they call fun . . . those kids never mess with the homosexuals cause a lot of them are rough . . . yeah they're demonstratin in the streets for their rights to marry one another . . . a woman marryin a woman, a guy marryin a guy . . . hell! I don't know why they wanna do that . . . I wouldn't get married . . . too many bills too many problems . . . now I don't mean that I don't wanna be around a buddy . . . I just mean I don't want no wife . . . ya know some of them women homosexuals are just as strong as men . . . one time I was in this bar and one of them women was sittin next to me she says: Hey buy me a drink . . . so I bought her one and then she tells me to buy her another one . . . I said Hell no. No woman's gonna take advantage of me . . . then the bartender leaned over and said: You better watch it she's a dyke and the woman said: Yeah I'm a dyke. So I bought her a drink . . . ya gotta watch it cause some of them are really rough . . .

The switchmen don't give ya any trouble . . . they only give the winos trouble. The winos and tramps who are hungry give ya the most trouble. Ya got all kinds of heads ridin these days . . . ya got pillheads, hopheads, jesus . . . they try to catch you asleep or drunk . . . then they hit ya over the head . . . that's when ya have trouble. I can't stand them winos. I know I look like a wino when I need a shave but I ain't one. Who needs to get wrapped up in wine all the money it takes to keep on gettin it. No not me . . . I just move around stop here or there at a mission to eat and clean up. The mission over in St. Paul is real nice . . . you fellas oughta come out with me . . . you'll get yourselves a good meal and a night's sleep. Well here's where I get off. Listen when I jump can ya throw my pack down right after me? it'll save me walkin all the way back to pick it up . . . and make sure ya jump before ya get to the switchyards . . . they got guys watchin from the towers . . .

Man on Second Avenue
2:00 A.M.

NEW YORK CITY

This guy I know was walking with a friend of his around West Street and they had gone into one of the bars and had a beer and after they were walking down the street when this car from Jersey cruised by . . . kids come around all the time throwin bottles and screamin *Queer* and then takin off . . . so this car cruised by real slow and some kid leans out the window sayin Suck my dick and my friend gave him the finger and said something. All of a sudden the car slams on the brakes and five kids come piling out and start kickin the shit out of my friend. For the next ten minutes about a hundred guys come out of the bars and from around the corner and surround these five kids beatin the shit outta my friend . . . his friend took off right away and later my friend found out that he had just run home didn't even bother calling the cops or nothing and all these guys crowding around watching five guys beatin up one guy and none of them said or did a thing . . . my friend said that they stomped on his head and chest and broke a lot of his ribs . . . at one point he got up and tried to break through the crowd but the kids got him by the hair and pulled him back in and he said it got to the point where he could hardly feel them hitting him they were jumping up and down on his head and arms and legs and finally he said he remembers jumping up and plowing through the crowd and running . . . his face was just a puddle of blood . . . the kids chased after him but he ran faster and faster through the streets and outta the neigh-borhood and he kept running till he collapsed somewhere on some street . . . later he woke up in the hospital and found out that he had been out for about five or six days. The doc-tors told him that he was found by the cops unconscious on West Street surrounded by a bunch of guys . . . apparently he had hallucinated the whole thing of getting up and run-ning away . . . he had never gotten up . . . the kids from Jer-sey got away too . . .

Boy in Trailer Park

COLLINSVILLE, ILLINOIS

I was makin this trip once . . . hitching from Detroit to Saginaw . . . I was hitching all day hoping some guy who picked me up would want to get it on . . . I had these fantasies of meeting someone really nice to make the trip something great . . . I finally got picked up by this one guy who used to live in Minneapolis and as we were riding along we were talking about politics and street stuff like what was going on with prostitutes and hustlers and all that . . . I told him that I didn't think they should arrest hustlers cause they weren't really doing anything fucked up and that I knew some hustlers myself and they were sensitive people. He gave me this funny kind of look and we started talkin about sexual repression and gay politics and after a while he pulled over to a highway rest stop and we both went in to take a piss. He stood in the booth next to me and stared at my face, you know gave me the eye, so a few minutes later we got back into the car and rode a while more. He said he lived in a small town just below Saginaw and asked me if I'd like to spend a few hours over at his place . . . he'd cook me a nice meal and if I wanted I could spend the night and he'd drive me up to Saginaw the next morning. I said Yeah and we pulled down this dirt road past all these broken-down farms and wheat fields and it was getting into late afternoon and the sunlight was really beautiful on the roads. We pulled into the driveway of this tiny farmhouse two stories tall and went inside. He had this dog tied up in the back a huge dog with long black fur . . . so after we get inside I'm waiting for him to like seduce me . . . see I never seduced anyone in my life I always let them seduce me . . . and he was much older than I was so it was awkward for me to even consider it. But he didn't make a move so I started thinking maybe I had figured him all wrong and I wished I had kept hitching instead of going home with him . . . anyway he went in and took a shower and after he came out I took a shower and after I shaved I came out in my underwear and he said: Ya wanna see the upstairs? so I said Okay and he took me upstairs. He told me he didn't really use the upstairs but for guests, that the dog hung out up there all the time. He took me into this little room that had an old bed in it and the sunlight was coming across the fields and through the window and it was really incredible the way it was shining in there. He told me I could lie down on the bed . . . he was real nervous when he said that . . . I lay down in my underwear and he just stood around tying his hands in knots. I started getting a hard-on and he couldn't help but notice it . . . he got all red and started to leave the room and said: Well, I'll leave ya alone and you can do whatever you want. I said: Hey, don't go stick around and he stood there all red in the face and looked uncomfortable . . . and I surprised myself by saying: Why don't you lay down next to me? he took off his shoes and lay down next to me all stiff like a desert mummy and after a few seconds I started running my hand down his side. He did the same and I slowly took off his clothes and then my own and we made love . . . it was real silent and slow ... the sun was coming in like the second coming of christ ... he was really awkward like he didn't have much experience and when it was over we both lay there for about an hour not saying anything to each other. Then he got up and went downstairs and took another shower. When I came down the phone rang and he answered it and it turned out he was on the board of the town, he was a high school teacher and they needed him for some kind of emergency meeting. So he split in his car and said he'd be back as soon as the meeting was over. I sat downstairs on the couch and the sun was slowly moving behind the hills. The place was incredibly quiet, just this high whine of insects in the fields and an occasional car passing by the house. Total silence and I had nothing to do but sit there and after an hour I was totally faded out just waiting ... didn't move for about three hours and there were these giant balls of dog hair that came from upstairs they were the size of softballs. They would get moved out of one of the upstairs rooms and slowly ride down the hallway and come silently down the long staircase and roll past me on the floor and disappear beneath the chair or couch. For three hours as the sun went down these fucking hair balls were coming down the stairs like one every ten or fifteen minutes ... and I couldn't move ... there was absolutely nothing that I could think of to do ... just waiting for this guy to come back from the town board meeting. I was crazy by the time he showed up ... I talked him into driving me to Saginaw that night and he did ...

The Waterfront

2:00 A.M.

NEW YORK CITY

was walking into the wind on the waterfront, past dark streets and the frames of rain-swept factories, listening to the sound of clipped heels on broken sidewalks. There had been a fire in the neighborhood recently . . . some old hotel burned down killing a tiny baby, some faceless name in the papers, and here it was, suddenly, a building with large stalactites hanging from its iron fire escape. The entire facade of the place was covered in a dull gleaming ice, bricks having long ago tumbled down to the sidewalk and a slight smoke still rolling from the ledges even now weeks after the fact. Far along the waterfront walkways were large ships with steel meshes of stacks and poles and lights burning effortlessly in the night. I could see stars through the upper stories of the hotel windows. A police car was idling nearby to ward off looters.

I saw a figure seated on a bench near the river. A young tough about twenty-three, wearing a thin jacket with the collar turned up against the cold winds. He had a ragged head of hair, coarse muscles pressing against the arms of his jacket, a pair of old work pants that looked smooth and warm. As I passed him sitting in a pool of light he lifted his head, a smile bruised his lips, throwing shadows. His nose looked like it had been damaged with a blow. He spit into his hands and rubbed them together for warmth. One hand slid down over his legs and nestled in the curve of his crotch. He smiled again and asked for a cigarette. I had a sealed pack on me and when I fished it out of my pocket, tore off the wrapper, and extended it towards him he said, Nah, man, you first. It's bad luck to take a man's first cigarette. I laughed and sat down next to him. He slid his hand down to his crotch again after lighting up with the end of my cigarette. He smiled and reached into his jacket pocket and slid out a small envelope of weed and some papers. I watched his hands as he attempted to roll: they were weathered, red and tough dark skin stretched over his fingers and squared knuckles. He had difficulty rolling, he'd been out in the cold too long.

You're a nice-lookin dude, y'know? he murmured. I'd love to get some of your skin. And he reached over pulling one of my hands onto his crotch. It stayed there after he took his hand away to continue rolling. I come all the way the fuck out here from Rockaway . . . been walking around for a long, long time. He smiled again, his eyes like slits. I felt a weakness in the pit of my stomach, my left leg started to jump. I could sense the distances this guy had traveled, not in terms of time and geography so much as an accumulation of experiences. When I become weary, these scenes, tense or sordid, become a soft mattress where I can lay my bodyless self down to drift. This guy was no angel. He kept spilling the weed into his lap so I took the papers from him and rolled one myself. It looked like a fat garden slug.

We got up and walked over to the railing separating us from the river, looked down upon it as we smoked, and I saw this tiny figure of a man in work clothes walking through the vast darkness of a five-acre asphalt dock towards a ship anchored on the rough currents. I watched him cover a large area of the walkway, moving along almost without step: it looked effortless like papers skidding on a current of air above pavements. I felt the weed hitting fast and waved away the joint as it was passed to me. Hey man . . . I come all the way from Rockaway to put some reefer to ya and you gonna say no? puff on it a while. I took it from his thick fingers and felt a warmth spread up from my belly. There was a slowness to his movements, he was beautiful. I could see the rough surface of his neck and the vein running down like a cord and disappearing beneath the collar of his shirt. He told me he had come out of the navy a few months back, dishonorable discharge because he was caught swiping some money from another man's footlocker. They beat the shit outta me first, ten guys on me but I cracked this sucker's teeth before they put me down. . . . The tiny man beside the ship began walking the illuminated gangplank in motions that took him up and towards us for a while and then another turn and away from us, going further into darkness. After a minute a thin line of light appeared on the side of the ship as he pulled open a door that had been buried in shadows. He disappeared through it, pulling it closed behind him. Listening carefully I could hear a tiny clink in the distance. I felt light-headed, blood moving fast within my chest, my temples throbbing like the bellies of small birds. His hand slid down and buried itself beneath my coat, around my waist and back. His neck was dirty, I could see lines on it as we passed under a lamp-post. We descended into the shadows of a ramp leading down to an abandoned playground, trees catching headlights and casting skeletal lines like X rays against the brick wall of an outhouse that had long ago been chained shut. They had once found some guy down there naked and tied up with his own shirt and belt, his wallet and valuables gone. Time was eas-

ing out. I saw images of my arms in the faint light, the rough-
ness of bricks making up the wall this guy was leaning on,
the curve of his hard fingers around the nape of my neck.
He was making a rough attempt to caress me. He leaned back
in an arched position, his mouth opened and a faint sigh
issued forth. I leaned over and kissed his neck and he laughed,
like in a drunken confusion of contempt and embarrassment.
I took it as embarrassment and felt myself growing hard. You
ain't sick are you? I stopped for a moment, realized he meant
VD and said no, slowly undoing his trousers. He squatted
down motioning me towards him with a single wave of his
hand. I rubbed my palms around the base of his neck over
and over, feeling the bristle of his skin against the sensitive
undersides of my wrists, smoothing down his jacket, over his
hard shoulders and muscles. He buried his face under my
shirt and rose upwards like an enormous fisted hand, his
tongue easing out between slightly parted lips so I could feel
the coolness of a breeze follow his motions. He stood up,
his arms swinging, and awkwardly embraced me. I fell into
him and he tugged at my pants till they came apart and he
worked a cold hand down into the back of my shorts. Nice
and smooth . . .

In the ledge of that playground, with thousands of cars blindly
swinging past, with the sense of my years circling around my
forehead, this guy turned me around pressing himself bodily
against me, his arms around my shoulders and neck, his hands
flat against my chest, nuzzling my earlobe and neck with his
warm breath, he entered me and breathed hard and rubbed
his hands down my sides and said he wished it were summer so he could stay out all night and I knew he probably
hadn't slept indoors for at least a week. As we both came he
fell back against the wall, his arms to the sides like he'd been

crucified and was delirious in the last intoxicating moments of it like St. Sebastian pierced with the long reeds of arrows, silhouetted against a night full of clouds opening up, revealing stars and a moon. We felt like figures adrift, like falling comets in old comic-book adventure illustrations. I thought how science texts never reveal how far the body would go for a sense of unalterable chance and change, something outside the flow of regularity: streets, job routines, sleepless nights on solitary damp mattresses.

I leaned towards him to see if he was alright. He thrust out a hand and pushed me backwards roughly. Piss, he murmured and a clear stream of it jetted out missing my shoe by inches. I watched as he slowly whizzed into the dim light, afterwards he buttoned up his pants and asked me which way the train station was. I led him up to the streets feeling dizzy, saw myself with him in the rough woods of that coastal dream I'd always had of losing myself from the general workings of the world: no Robinson Crusoe but some timeless place where the past was forgettable and there was just some guy with a tough stomach to lie against, and I could listen to his heart-beat sounding through his trembling skin. We passed an old woman sitting on her stoop talking to a cop on a side street. They jimmied open a door . . . and suddenly they were in. I marveled at the sound and pulled up my collar against the fresh blasts of winter wind.

From the Diaries
of a Wolf Boy

'm still a piece of meat like something in the Fourteenth Street markets swinging from stinking hooks in the blurry drag queen dusk. Maybe a hundred dollars to my name, no place to live, and I can't hustle anymore. I'm trying to keep my body beyond the deathly fingers of my past but I'm fucked up bad never learned shit, how to create structures other than chaos. I'm attracted to chaos because of all the possibilities and I don't have to choose any of them or die frozen inside one but right now all I know is that I am tired, bone and brain tired. I woke up in this guy's bed in the middle of the night and realized not a whole lot had changed since I got off the streets. He was an alcoholic doctor I'd known on and off over a handful of years and he let me live with him for the last couple of weeks cooking me upper-class meals in return for me fucking him legs over my shoulders like a video stud. He could have gone on forever like this but the distinct sensation of being made of glass, of being completely invisible to him, was growing and curving like a cartoon wave. I feel so fucking dark I don't even have the energy to throw myself off a building or bridge. Now he's starting to come home slam-down drunk banging into walls moaning and crying falling down murmuring: Fuck me my lovely. I told him one night he needed some help and he responded by bringing home a hustler from West Street and I ended up sleeping on the living room floor.

The doctor takes me on a week's vacation in his station wagon up to the coast of Maine. No license but I'm driving the almost deserted interstate north. I haven't slept for about two days and feel sort of drugged, the hypnotic lines of the dawn's highway wavering like an unraveled hypnotist's disk. It's kind of beautiful the foliage on the shoulders still illuminated by the tungsten lamps blip blip blip. The doctor vaguely woke up and his hand drifted over the armrest between us and slid over my leg slowly back and forth till I got a hard-on. Then his sleepy fingers unbuttoned my trousers and he leaned over taking my dick in his mouth. There was a car way ahead of us and another way behind; beacons of headlights were circling the hills and the sky was turning still and black, night being pushed up through the sky over the car by a quiet surfacing day. My whole body stiffened with my hands on the wheel. I had a hard-on for thirty miles moving my hips up and down finally shooting into his mouth, surprised as a lone car overtook us and sped past causing me to realize I'd slowed down to fifteen miles per hour.

He rented a motel room somewhere on the breezy oceanside. An oddly beautiful coastline but I knew this was temporary so I didn't let myself buy into it. I went for a walk while he slept and climbed through the craggy rock postcard views among postcard families and vacationing heterosexuals, drifted away from the sand and up onto this mammoth asphalt parking lot bordering the motel. This guy, young and handsome in an indefinable way, with short brown hair, a pair of dark shorts that revealed muscular legs slightly browned from weather and sun, a ruddy color to his forehead and cheeks and nose, coasted up on a bicycle and stopped short a distance away checking me out. I was walking under this long canopied bench area so I sat on one of the empty seats, folded my arms over the back of the bench and laid my head on it staring at him sideways. He rolled a little closer and dismounted, standing next to his bike hands thrust deep into pockets for a while. He finally moved towards me one more time then tossed back the hair from over his eyes, a boyish gesture suggestive of a remote past, school days, something that still makes me weak in the knees. He said: Hey, hello. I straightened up and said: How's it going? He gestured okay with his head and then said: Where do ya go for fun around here? I told him I just got into town and didn't know nothing. I felt that blush in my chest as we talked stupid talk never quite revealing our queerness to each other but somehow wordlessly generating volumes of desire like some kind of sublanguage that makes you want to splash into it even with all its tensions. He continued loose conversation watching me closely for reactions to his coded words and then finally seemed to abandon it all and said: You want to get together later? We made a date for 11 P.M. at the same spot and I walked away wondering how to handle the doctor.

The doctor started drinking after dinner and I encouraged him to go to bed. He finally fell asleep around 10:45 and I slipped from between the sheets, put on my clothes, and fished the room key out of his pocket, every movement noiseless until the barely audible click of the door. I walked to the bench area overlooking the ocean and stood around. The night was heavy, the water indiscernible in the darkness. The tide was way out so it was just this screen of grainy blackness that contained the rushing hollow sounds of waves crashing way out there. Every so often a lone car would swing to the lot, its headlights illuminating one patch of ocean in a field of circular light, and beyond that I could see the low caps of broken waves spreading in towards shore, lit as if by luminous microbes. I walked down to the sand into the darkness to see how far I could go before I touched water, leaving behind the cars turning round and round and the windows of the motel along the beach with rectangles of burning orange light and the flap of banners and flags as the staff hoisted them on poles for the holidays.

I got close to the water's edge when an old ghost of a man materialized with his open palms stretching out towards me. I heard a murmur: Want some action? I turned and walked to the opening of the bay along the coastline, climbing the boulders to the back end of the parking lot. Walking to the bench area two local toughs: *Hey yo!* came up fast behind me their arms dangling at their sides like whirligigs. Both were kind of sexy but dangerous. One guy with close-cropped hair and a red face said: Any women out here tonight? then they came up on me on both sides spinning their heads from looking for witnesses. I became as charming as possible: Cigarette? As they took one a car spun in the lot illuminating all of us and I took that moment to tip towards the headlights and lose myself among the parked cars. I circled back to the benches and the young guy I'd met earlier was sitting on the hood of his car. He told me to get in and we drove out into the town, parking behind a deserted bank and walking through the streets looking for a bar. He wanted to drink some beers. His name was Joe and he was in town for the naval reserves, a two-week training with a few days off in between.

* * *

There were no regular bars around just a couple of queer joints with heavy cover charges and pounding disco, so we ended up walking a couple miles down a dark road talking about ourselves and the distances we'd been. We turned back to his car. The gearheads were out in their pickup trucks whizzing around the curves of the small streets. One truck sped by a club we were approaching and white ugly distended faces blew out of the side windows: *We hate queers!* I turned to him: Let's go somewhere. Okay? Yeah, he said: We really should. There's got to be a place we can just sit down and have a drink and talk. I was wondering if I had this guy wrong; if that's all he wanted was talking company. I was already drawn in by the movements of his chest and belly beneath his shirt, his arms and the outline of his thighs in his trousers. I turned to him in the darkness behind the bank and said: Well, what I really meant was that I want to lie down with you at some point. Tonight. In fact the sooner the better; I can't stay out all night. He laughed: For sure for sure. We got into the car and I was feeling nervous. He startled me by reaching his arm out, encircling my neck and pulling my face over his. His mouth opened slow and he kissed me for a few seconds. He drew away leaving his hand curved around the nape of my neck and smiled, leaned back in for another kiss, and then drew away again. He patted me on the leg and turned the key in the ignition.

He had this shitty piece of plastic that he'd fashioned into a tent strung between two trees in a forest of firs. It was some rarely used campground way up in the hills, no lights just dirt roads among the trees. The car twisted its way along illuminating a pitched tent or rusting trailer. He finally swung

in between some trees and came to a stop snapping the headlights off. He left his door open a bit softly casting light on
nearby trees. His tent billowed in the slight breeze.

We stood in the dark kissing for a while, then he went
to the back of the car and got an old sleeping bag out from
the trunk and spread it under the tent. He closed the car door
extinguishing the interior light and turned on a tiny flashlight,
lying on the ground between us. We struggled to get our
clothes off we were so blasted from a bowl of pot he pro-
duced as we drove up the hillside. We were trying to pull off
our pants standing on one leg, tipping over and making crashing noises in the bushes. I was completely disoriented but
he grabbed onto my arm pulling me into the opening of the
tent his skin so warm. We couldn't stop tasting each other's
mouths, changing back and forth in different positions, lying
on top of each other, moving down and licking each other's
arms and bellies and chests. At some point I was hovering
over him in a push-up position leaning down drawing my
tongue over the wet curves of his armpits when an intense
light swept over the tent. I felt like we were in the path of a
searchlight. A lot of noise, shouts, and the slamming of car
doors. I froze with my mouth on his chest and then the light
disappeared.

At about two in the morning he dropped me off outside the
hotel and we exchanged addresses. I entered the room as
quietly as I could and saw the doctor still passed out in the
bed. I had that rude perfume of sex all over me and needed
to take a shower. I passed through the darkened room into
the bathroom and closed the door, stripping off my clothes
and hitting the light switch. I was in front of an enormous
mirror that reflected an image of my pale white body cov-

ered in dozens of thick red welts. Mosquitoes. Everywhere. I
took a hot shower, soaped off, and finally crawled into bed
without waking the doctor. The next morning the welts were
gone. Everything was casual and we left the motel and drove
up the coast.

My life was falling apart. A hustler moved in and I spent a
week's worth of nights on the living room floor. I scavenged
for leftovers in the refrigerator rather than sit for sullen meals
at the dining table. I'd wake up early and leave for the day
coming back only after the doctor and his boy were asleep.
He left me a couple of angry letters taped to the refrigerator
saying he didn't like the ghost routine and that he thought I
should give him his set of keys back. I'd been writing Joe for
a while and asked if I could come up for a visit. He wrote
back saying he had a four-day break coming up the next
week. I called him long distance and he gave me instructions
to some small town in Massachusetts and said he'd meet me
at the bus station. I packed a small shopping bag and left
without saying anything to the doctor. I didn't know what I
was doing or where I was going I was just leaning into a drift
and sway that I hoped would set me down gentle. I walked
around the streets until five in the morning around the East
Village and sat on a bench near St. Mark's Church watching
dawn coming up. A pale, depressed queen sat down next to
me and eventually invited me to his place nearby. It was a
filthy room in a tenement with lots of dirty bed sheets and
clothes. I stayed there a week till I caught the bus to Ludlow.

He met me at the station and drove to some queer bar on the
outskirts of a city. We stood in the dark near a cigarette
machine and hardly spoke, grinning at each other and suck-

ing on cold bottles. Later he drove us back to his apartment complex where he shared a small place on the second floor with his brother. We went for a walk in the back fields and woods down a dirt road where a fat 'coon kept trying to beat the cars to get across. We followed rusting steel railroad tracks long ago abandoned, reddish brown and swallowed up by the dense undergrowth. We pushed through thick nets of trees and bushes catching our feet on vines past a house with a howling yard dog behind a storm fence, through some forest with a steep incline tumbling towards a river. Further on we came to tracks that continued on a trestle bridge which went over small rapids that merged into a vast smooth curve suddenly broken up on more rocks creating a whooshing spill towards the west. Watching the trees dipping down towards the banks we were forty or fifty feet up in the air tightroping these tracks with nothing but rotting steel stanchions holding us up. There were sounds of leftover fireworks somewhere in the distance, huge bullhead clouds, some rosy from the disappearing sun, others dark and bruise-colored drifting heavily overhead. We sat on a girder, the water rushed below giving us the sensation that we were moving at high speeds through the quiet and dying world.

He pulled a little bowl of pot from his pants and lit up. I had a difficult time not staring at his arms and torso, he left his T-shirt back at his place. I was falling, like from the portal of a plane way up in the skies. He had the kind of sexy grace that you want to swim in, currents warm and breathing. In those years I fell in love easily: gestures of an arm, the simple line of a vein in the neck, the upturning of a jaw in dim light, the lines of a body beneath clothing, the clear light of the eyes when your faces almost touch. We talked about flying saucers, whether it's some kind of psychic reality for those who claim abduction or whether it's some kind of psychic schism that people have experienced. I was slowly leaning towards him and without any reason suddenly kissed his bare shoulder. He kind of wigged, pulled back in vague shock: Uh uh. Don't ever do that. There's people around here.

Two days later at around midnight he stepped out of his bed and squatted next to where I lay on a sleeping bag on the floor of his room. He was wearing shorts and he pulled his dick out the leg part and bounced it against my lips. We hadn't mentioned sex since I arrived. We got into something quiet and slow, came, and then he slid back into his bed and fell asleep.

I was feeling dislocated, my money was going to run out fairly quick from fast-food meals and occasional beers. The feeling of dislocation was really about dreaming too much in this guy's movements. There was nothing ahead of me but a return to the streets of New York unless there's something called love but it probably doesn't exist except in the my-thologies we're fed in the media or by lying to ourselves over time. It's not only the urge to climb inside someone's skin and fuse in the rivers of their blood; it's wanting to leave the face of the planet, our bodies rolling against each other in the cool spacious sky. But this guy couldn't verbalize any-thing that touched his sexuality; he had a look of pain when I strayed near words so I slid back into my solitary drift and waited till his hands began to move towards me.

We were going to go swimming so he lent me a pair of cut-offs which I put on, slightly self-conscious about my hospi-tal-white legs. His legs were darker, sturdier, that's what I recall about first meeting him on the windswept coast, late afternoon beneath the flapping canvas awnings and the lines of his muscular thighs and calves. We were in his two-door car stopping outside of town to pick up a six-pack and then onto the interstate. We went many miles further, finally swinging onto this small asphalt road, then onto an even smaller road that climbed up through trees and into hillsides. He was picking up some kid who wanted to come with us. (Telephone call: Is your mother home? Well, then, meet us on the rock near the road.) (Hanging up the phone: He's really worried about his mom or sister seeing him going out with other guys.) We pulled onto this fucked-up asphalt strip that rolls vertically up another hillside, made a curve and there's this young kid maybe seventeen sitting on a large white boulder lodged in the green lawn. He looked vaguely Indian, and he also had muscular legs, a baby-hair mustache almost transparent on his lip. (Later that evening: Yeah I met him outside a bar in Springfield. They carded him and he had to stay outside. We camped out in his backyard a couple times . . . Yeah I slept with him once. The first night I met him we talked for a long long time. He didn't have a ride home so we got in my car, ran out of gas the needle on empty just outside his home. His mother works in a hospital, father dead. We spent the night in his house no one home.)

Down by the lake right off the road in a dirt patch we parked with the windows open and a slight breeze easing through. The kid was rolling a meticulous joint on a cardboard cover of a shoe box; gypsy moths, hundreds of them, beat soundlessly against the trunks of trees, some flying over into the windshield of the car, climbing inside, around the dashboard, on our legs, leaving behind a blond powder. Someone's ugly poodle, hairless, almost gray skin, was tied to a tree shivering in the tall grass. We could hear sounds of splashing and ripple currents drifting nearby. I was smoked up to the point of getting stupid. I got out of the car and drifted to the water's edge. I walked ahead of them into the lake with my eyes focused on the horizon like a happy zombie, steady, smoothly upright, I moved forward into the dreamy nothingness with the waters riding up around my waist and further up around my chest, shocking my armpits, I was far from shore without my glasses; everything took on that indistinct look like water cascading over a window, just wobbly form and light and color. Without my glasses color seems to fade because there are no true lines to contain it, it mixes with things and rides outside its surfaces, no density to anything in the world but what I feel beneath my feet.

I dive in the water and swim for the longest while beneath its surface slow and quiet. I'm aquatic, surrounded by silence, everything gray beneath my eyelids, feeling like I'm aware for the first time of my arms and hands and kicking legs and what they all mean. I lay sideways on the water's surface seeing pale bodies of strangers moving waist high on the shoreline far away.

In the shallows of the lake I walk on my hands, digging into the sand. Further out it's silt so soft and deep you know it's black and rich; my feet sink up to the ankles. It's a texture that's like the inside of a body when your fingers go wandering. I pulled smooth objects to the surface, some kind of freshwater mussels. He's doubtful when I tell him so I toss one to him and he's amazed. Later he holds it against the top of a wooden fencepost and slams it with a rock cracking the shell to bits, which he pulls apart revealing tan flesh. I pick up my little camera off the backseat and take his picture. He gets embarrassed: You just take a picture of me? Yeah, I said. Just of you talking. (Not of your beautiful chest which I'd love to spit on and rub my dick over.) The car radio is on and the announcer says: The worst riots in England in memory; worst civilian damage since World War II.

Later we drive the kid back home, up the small darkening road of the hillside into the blue shadows of evening. The house is softly illuminated from behind by a back porch light. The kid gets agitated: Uh oh . . . my mother's probably home . . . uh . . . just let me off here and if ya can turn around in someone else's drive . . . I didn't leave that light on . . . she's probably home. We say good night and he whispers: Joe . . . call you later in the week. He turns and runs across the lawn disappearing into the shadows of the porch, screen door squeaking and the bowwow of a dog.

His brother has buddies hanging out in their apartment; they might spend the night since it's heading towards the week-end. He wants sex with me really bad all of a sudden. He's trying to get a motel room so we're on the interstate driving miles and miles. Finally he spots a Holiday Inn. I wait in the car as he goes inside to register. I'm sitting there for a long time feeling this melancholy circle around me. Couldn't tell exactly what it was, part of it I guess was being outside New York City in a slow place with air and grass and bodies of water to lie down in. Some of it was the growing tension leaving soon almost broke and no place to live. Death was a smudge in the distance. I don't know what exactly I mean by that but lying down inside this cradle of arms in my head was sometimes all I wanted. Sometimes I wonder what planet I got dropped off from; what foreign belly did I get birthed from. This shit is painful, it's like being on a raft way out in the middle of a sea completely alone. I wave my hands in front of me, I know I'm not invisible, why are my thoughts so fucking loud? I'm lost in a world that's left all its mythologies behind in the onward crush of wars and civilization, my body traveling independent of brushes with life and death, no longer knowing what either means anymore. I'm so tired of feeling weary and alien, even my dreams look stupid to me. They belong to another world, another century, maybe another gender that fits the codes of all this shit. I don't know.

He comes back visibly upset, swings into the car through the driver's open window, slumps back: Shit. How could I be so fucking stupid? The clerk asked me if I lived nearby and I told him where and he goes: We have a policy not to rent to nobody who lives within a thirty-mile radius of here.

He was upset. I put my hand on his leg and said: Look, don't let the asshole get you down. So what? Let's look for another place or else forget it and go for a ride. (I really wanted to try to fuck him.) We drove onto the highway again and rode for a while in silence. He pulled into a Ramada Inn. He got a room. Everything was calm again. He took a six-pack of beer from the trunk along with a carton of photographs and albums from his days at sea. It was a standard motel room with double beds and cheap thick white curtains, a sink with glasses wrapped in wax paper and a color television with air conditioner humming behind it.

We're sitting on one of the beds, our shirts off, shoes and socks lying scattered across the floor, our legs resting together and stray hands smoothing down each other's sides and chests. We're looking at his notebooks filled with Kodak pictures of faraway places and naval scenes of boy sailors passing the equator. Mop wigs and overloaded halter tops and string skirts and underwear of different colors. Some of the photos look like a drunken fashion show with sturdy-legged guys with balloons or cloth tits beneath their T-shirts, sort of like a hula nightmare but more sexy. In other pictures they're dressed like canines, on all fours with sheets of paper and cardboard curved and strung around their faces with Magic Marker lines drawn like grinning dogs. One Filipino guy has a white T-shirt with a pirate's skull drawn on his chest. Another guy is dressed like a hound dog bitch with eight fat

papier-mâché tits dragging on the deck. There were other
pictures of him with all his friends, bare-chested waist high
in a foreign sea with delicate pink and white flowered leis
around their necks. I put my hand casually on his butt and
he jerks away. Anyone ever put their hands on your ass? I
ask. He makes a disgusted noise: That's fucking gross; I'd
never put my dick in somebody's ass and I'd never let somebody try that with me . . . makes me sick to think about it.
Same way I'd never be in a relationship with a guy, maybe a
girl but never a guy . . . it just ain't . . . uh . . . normal . . . it
just doesn't make any sense. I don't mind playing around here
or there but not a relationship . . . No way.

Sometimes I wish I could blow myself up. Wrap a belt of
dynamite around my fucking waist and walk into a cathedral
or the Oval Office or the home of my mother and father. I'm
in the last row of the bus, the seven other passengers are
clustered like flies around the driver in the front. I can see
his cute fuckable face in the rearview mirror. I lean back and
tilt my head so all I see are the clouds in the sky. I'm looking
back inside my head with my eyes wide open. I still don't
know where I'm going; I decided I'm not crazy or alien. It's
just that I'm more like one of those kids they find in remote
jungles or forests of India. A wolf child. And they've dragged
me into this fucking schizo-culture, snarling and spitting and
walking around on curled knuckles. They're trying to give
me a damp mattress to sleep on in a dark corner when all I
really want is the rude perfume of some guy's furry under-
arms and crotch to lean into. I'll make guttural sounds and
stop eating and drinking and I'll be dead within the year. My
eyes have always been advertisements for an early death.

CPSIA information can be obtained
at www.ICGtesting.com
Printed in the USA
BVHW03s0211100418
512917BV00001B/32/P